gee whiz

gee whiz

Jane Smiley

with illustrations by Elaine Clayton

ALFRED A. KNOPF
NEW YORK

THIS IS A BORZOI BOOK PUBLISHED BY ALFRED A. KNOPF

Visit us on the Web! randomhouse.com/kids

Educators and librarians, for a variety of teaching tools, visit us at
RHTeachersLibrarians.com

Library of Congress Cataloging-in-Publication Data
Smiley, Jane.
Gee Whiz / Jane Smiley ; with illustrations by Elaine Clayton. — 1st ed.
p. cm.
(The horses of oak valley ranch; bk. 5)
Summary: Soon after her yearling, Jack, begins working with professional trainers at a nearby ranch, Abby Lovitt takes responsibility for a very large, very smart, and very curious retired racehorse named Gee Whiz.
ISBN 978-0-375-86969-3 (trade) — ISBN 978-0-375-96969-0 (lib. bdg.) —
ISBN 978-0-375-98533-1 (ebook)
[1. Horses—Training—Fiction. 2. Ranch life—California—Fiction.
3. Family life—California—Fiction. 4. Christian life—Fiction.
5. California—History—1950—Fiction.] I. Clayton, Elaine, ill. II. Title.
PZ7.S6413Gee 2013
[Fic]—dc23
2012024370

The text of this book is set in 11.5-point Goudy.

Printed in the United States of America
October 2013
10 9 8 7 6 5 4 3 2 1
First Edition

gee whiz

Rodeo Rigging and Strap

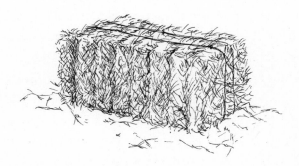

Hay Bale

gee whiz

Rodeo Rigging and Strap

Hay Bale

Chapter 1

MY PLAN WAS TO LET BLUE AND JACK PLAY FOR TEN OR FIF-
teen minutes, then to catch Blue and tack him up, then to
ride him in the arena while Jack trotted and wandered about.
That way, I would get two horses done in the time it would
normally take for one, and I would also get to watch Jack
while riding Blue. I had already put Jack in the arena; now I
opened the gate again and walked in with Blue. Jack came
trotting over to us, his neck arched and his ears pricked. His
tail was arched, too. I took off Blue's halter and they sniffed
each other, then Blue trotted away as if he were interested in
every other thing in the arena but Jack. Jack trotted behind
him.

Jack decided to investigate the cones. He went over to

one and sniffed it, then snorted and reared a bit, then sniffed it again. He trotted around it, and then stopped and looked at the cone beside it. Blue continued to ignore him—he was looking for bits of grass under the arena fence, walking along with his head down and his nose to the ground. I went to the center of the arena and started straightening the poles that were lying there. It was the last day of November, a cool, breezy day. The grass was beginning to turn green—it was bright-looking and appetizing, but I wondered if it had much flavor, since sometimes the horses spit it out. The quiet lasted for about a minute, then it was as if both horses had the same thought—"What's *he* doing?" They turned at the same time, trotted over to one another, and sniffed noses. All at once, Jack reared up and took off along the fence line, and in half a second, Blue went after him. I smiled and continued to push the poles—there were about twelve of them—closer together. The horses galloped for ten strides or so, bucking and squealing. Jack even reared up once, but when they came to the far end of the arena, they turned into real Thoroughbreds—they stopped acting up and started running, and by the time they were halfway down the far side, I knew they were having a race. I stood and stared.

Jack was on the outside and Blue was on the inside. I think it was the moment that they stretched their necks out and lengthened their stride that I began to worry, because, in fact, it did not look like they were playing—it looked like they cared. And unlike the training pen, which we sometimes put them in but was too small for them to get going, the arena was big enough for some speed but maybe small enough for trouble. A racetrack is a mile around. Not our arena. I looked toward the house. I didn't know if I wanted Mom to see what was happening and come out and stop it, or if I wanted Dad to show up and yell at me. The best would be Danny. Danny should appear and treat me like a kid and help me prevent these horses from killing themselves.

Because they were going fast. Long, hard strides, digging deep into the footing, neck and neck, as they say at the racetrack. Blue was slightly ahead, but Jack did not want to give up. He even whinnied his high whinny. Their manes and forelocks flew, the sand rose around their bellies, and they ran. Their ears were pinned. I counted the number of circuits they made—one, two, three—and with each circuit, I thought of about a zillion different bad things that might happen. At one point, Blue's foot slipped—he didn't fall down, but he might have, so I imagined that for a while. Or he might have bumped Jack into the fence rail. Or he might have crossed Jack's path and then they both could have gone down. Or there could be a hole or a depression in the sand that I didn't know about—stumble, fall. What an idiot I was to have put them in here together. I shouted, "Hey, Blue! Hey, Jack! Slow down! Hey, fellas! Hey, Blue! Blue! How are you?"

And Blue's ears flicked in my direction.

And Jack passed him.

Then they slowed down.

Then they trotted.

Then they tossed their heads and snorted.

Then Jack nipped at Blue and Blue nipped at Jack.

Then I saw how sweaty they were, and how hard they were breathing.

Then Blue turned and trotted over to me and Jack followed him.

They looked okay.

I said, "Thank you, Lord," just the way Dad would have. And I meant it.

I got Blue's halter off the gate and, since he had followed me, turned and put it on him right there, then I walked him around until he wasn't panting any longer. Jack, in the meantime, was rolling in the sand—down, up, walk to another spot; down, up, walk to another spot. He seemed very proud of himself.

And me, well, my anxiety faded away and all I could think about was how beautiful and free they had looked, their tails streaming and their muscles shimmering. It was the way it had been earlier in the fall, when a trainer, Ralph Carmichael, was in town. He trained the horses to jump by having them gallop in pairs, or even in groups, down a jumping chute. The first time you saw it, it seemed like dangerous chaos, but then you realized that the horses not only enjoyed it, they were smart about it. Once we'd let Blue do it a few times, he knew more about jumping than I had been able to teach him.

When I came in for supper, which was macaroni and cheese and green beans, but with a peach pie, Mom and Dad were acting funny, so I knew something was going on. Then, when I was passing through the hall to go upstairs to the bathroom, I saw that there was an opened envelope on the telephone stand, and it was from the Wheatsheaf Ranch in Texas.

It took about half a second for my heart to jump into my mouth, because that was the ranch where Warn Matthews lived. Most people would say that Jack, who was almost two, belonged to Mr. Matthews. Most people would say that Jack's dam, whom Dad had bought from a dealer in Oklahoma, had been stolen, so when she gave birth to a surprise foal out in our pasture, the foal belonged to Mr. Matthews, too, even though the mare colicked and died when he was a month old. Some people might say that although I adored Jack, I had to give him back. But Mr. Matthews didn't think like that. He said that since we bought the mare in good faith, and since we took good care of her and her foal, we would share him "for now." My problem was, I kept worrying about "later." My hand just about grabbed the envelope on its own, but the letter wasn't in the envelope. Mom or Dad probably had it in the kitchen. They were waiting for "the right moment."

I went upstairs, but I was back downstairs in a hurry. When I sat down at the table, the letter, a typewritten page, was sitting at my plate. I picked it up. Even though Mr. Matthews had been plenty nice to me, that didn't have to keep going. Sometimes people do things to you for your own good, and those things don't feel good at all. The letter read:

Dear Abby, Mark, and Sarah—

It has been a busy year around Wheatsheaf, especially on the horse-racing side. You may or may not know that our three-year-old Yardstick, by Bold Ruler out of our homebred mare Hot Spell, has had quite an exciting season—fourth in the Kentucky Derby, second in the

Preakness, then first in the Whitney and second to Buck-passer in the Travers. Of course, we would have preferred to win! But Yardstick has held up well, and should have a good year next year as a four-year-old. We have also been back and forth to Europe this year. We purchased an interest in a horse named Hill Rise, who looked as though he would be running in the Queen Elizabeth at Ascot and then the Arc. As it turned out, he didn't go to France, but his win at Ascot was incredibly exciting, especially since he was bred in California.

All of this is by way of an apology for not having kept in touch with you concerning the yearling "Jack," by Jaipur out of Alabama Lady. Yes, early in the summer, the Jockey Club informed us that after considerable debate, they have decided to allow Jack into the studbook. Although there is no definitive evidence that Jack is indeed Alabama Lady's colt, or that your mare was Alabama Lady, the breeding and foaling dates, along with the cir-cumstances of the theft and her appearance at By Golly Horse Sales, are sufficiently compelling to tip the scales in our favor. My guess is that they went back and forth about this matter for a good long while, but whatever happened, they have now decided to accept him. Being a gelding may have helped him, because they only have to let him race, and don't have to worry about offspring. Anyway, we must make up our minds what to do next.

Normally, a Thoroughbred born in January, as Jack was, goes into training in September of his second year—which would have been this past September—so that he can have a couple of races as a two-year-old. Around

6

Wheatsheaf, we don't press the two-year-olds very hard, but we have found that the ones who wait to run, for whatever reasons of health or circumstances, are harder to handle and are less likely to do well. My own theory is that three-year-olds are like kids in junior high—sassier and more rebellious—so you want your horses to have learned their job when they are still willing. Since we have our own training facility here, we can take it horse by horse, start them, and go on with them as we wish, and then we normally ship them to Kentucky and Arkansas to begin their racing careers. But I don't see how this will work with Jack. For one thing, he is not used to Texas weather, especially the humidity, and for another, my son Barry, whom you have not met, has gotten to know a fellow in your neighborhood who runs a well-respected training facility pretty much down the road from you called Vista del Canada. The man's name is Roscoe Pelham, he's an experienced horseman, and he'd like to have Jack over there.

The only other question that remains is what Jack's registered name will be. Some racehorse names are pretty ridiculous—I'm proud of "Yardstick" in a way, because lots of Bold Ruler horses have what I consider prideful names, but "Yappy" and "Buckaroo Banana" just seem a little silly to me. So we need to start thinking of something.

I hope this is good news for you, and that you and your horses, and Jack, of course, are all well and happy. Maybe sometime after the racing season, you folks can come down to Wheatsheaf for a little visit.

I look forward to hearing from you.

Warn Matthews

Mom said, "Doesn't Jake Morrisson shoe horses over at that place? Maybe Danny's actually been there."

Dad said, "You're thinking of Laguna Seca. Vista del Canada is the private place—don't know a thing about it, except that it is supposed to be very grand."

I said, "Jane might know some of those people. She talked about them once." Jane was the manager of a big stable on the coast where I rode in shows.

Dad said, "Those aren't the same ones, I'm sure." What he meant was, those aren't the people who tried to cheat us out of five thousand dollars right around the time that Mr. Matthews showed up and saved the day. But he looked worried, because what was the difference between one horse-racing gambler and another, really? I mean, he liked Mr. Matthews because he was a rancher, and they could talk cattle and cow horses. Or I thought that was why he looked worried, until he said, "I wonder what it costs."

Mom said, "I guess we'll find out."

Dad said, "We need to find out before we take the horse over there, is what I think."

I thought about my bank account—a hundred and six dollars. I wondered how long that would last, even if Mr. Matthews was splitting it with us. Dad said, "I'll write him back, and we'll pray on it." I saw that he was pretty reluctant to open the Bible and see what Scripture advised, and I didn't blame him.

Even though I had to get up early to get to the school bus, I couldn't help lying awake, wondering about sending Jack to a place that was "down the road," much less to Texas. I had pretty much forgotten about the fact that Mr. Matthews might want to do something with Jack—we hadn't heard from him all summer, and what with riding, and training Blue, and trying to figure out high school, I hadn't thought about the Jockey Club in months. Well, wasn't this a good thing? Yes, Jack *was* the son of Jaipur and the grandson of Nasrullah and Determine. But I sort of hoped that Dad would decide that it was too much money. (And how much would that be? The stables where the horse shows were, where Sophia Rosebury kept her horses, and where Blue had come from, charged a hundred dollars every month just for board, and that didn't include any training—board and breaking and training could be twice that.) Maybe Jack could stay home.

I rolled over, and of course what happens when you roll over is that you get another bad thought. Mr. Matthews was nice enough now, but if we decided that we didn't want Jack to go to Vista del Canada, maybe he could just say, "Okay, Texas it is," and Jack would have to go there. It was about at this point that I decided that I would write Mr. Matthews myself, and suggest that we keep Jack at home and Jem Jarrow could start him. Yes, that was a good idea, and I would think about the name later. I fell asleep. Jem Jarrow wore cowboy boots and worked at his brother's ranch, but he could train any horse to do anything.

That was Wednesday. Friday, we had a surprise. It was a pleasant surprise, but it was definitely a surprise. Dad and I were riding Mr. Tacker's five-year-old quarter horse gelding, Marcus, and our beautiful paint mare, Oh My, in the arena when a truck and trailer pulled up to the gate, and Danny got out of the passenger's side, opened the gate, let the rig through, and closed the gate. It was a nice two-horse trailer and a new truck—newer than ours. When it pulled up to the parking area beside the barn, a guy got out. He looked about Danny's age. He was wearing the usual stuff—jeans, cowboy hat, jean jacket. He and Danny came over to the fence, and he took off his hat. His hair popped up like it was made of springs. He dipped his head to us, and Danny said, "Dad, this is Jerry Gardino. Jerry, this is my dad, Mark Lovitt, and my sister, Abby. Jerry's looking for a place to keep his horse for a couple of months, and I knew you had room. There's nothing at Marble Ranch at the moment." Marble Ranch was the ranch where Danny worked and lived. Then, as if reading Dad's mind, Danny said, "Jerry knows that you charge seventy-five dollars per month with him supplying oats or corn."

Dad relaxed at once, and said, "The more the merrier."

Jerry Gardino gave us a smile, and it was a very big smile. It made you smile right back.

He said, "Thanks, Mr. Lovitt. I really appreciate this. The season's over, and Beebop needs a little time off. Danny says he'll get great care, and this place looks perfect. There's a spot up where I go to school, but no grass, and not much turnout. Hate to do that to a horse."

I dismounted, and Jerry cemented his good impression by saying, "That one's a beauty."

Dad leaned over and gave Oh My a pat and said, "Well, the black-and-white overo paint is fairly unusual, for sure, but look at this." I turned Oh My around so Jerry could see the question mark on her left side. He said, "Oh my." They always did.

Dad said, "What kind of horse do you have?"

"Oh, Beebop is a little bit of everything—Thoroughbred mixed with quarter horse mixed with sixteen other varieties maybe. Some mustang in there for sure. He's a bucking horse. I take him around to rodeos, and mostly he gets out from under 'em."

Danny said, "You should see the pictures."

The horse, when we unloaded him, was nice enough—a liver chestnut with a friendly eye, no white on him, and of medium height and build—just the sort of horse that a judge wouldn't look at twice. We put him in a stall with a nice pile of hay for the night, and Danny said he would come over with Jerry the next day and introduce him to the geldings. Then Mom came out and invited the two of them for supper, and by the fact that we were having fried chicken and mashed potatoes and gravy, it was clear that she had known about this all along.

Over supper, Danny and Jerry talked about our local rodeo in the summer. Danny had taken his horse, Happy, in a few roping classes, and Jerry, who had been standing by the railing, had admired her. He said, "She almost had you off that one time, remember that? She just spun and you were lucky to hang on."

Danny laughed. "Well, she's quick and she never saw a calf she didn't want to boss around." Jerry took Beebop to the rest of his appointments on the rodeo circuit, and Danny went back to work shoeing, and it was only when Jerry came over to Marble Ranch looking for a place for the winter that they had recognized each other. Mom asked Jerry where he was from, what his folks did, all that stuff that moms do, and Jerry said he was from San Francisco, his dad and his uncles were all butchers, he had grown up in Little Italy up there. . . .

Dad said, "You didn't grow up on a ranch?"

"Right downtown," said Jerry. "Four houses from the corner of Mason and Union."

I don't think I'd ever seen such a surprised look on my dad's face. Both Mom and Danny laughed.

He said, "And you've ridden bulls?"

"Not well," said Jerry. "But it was something I wanted to do all my life, from the first time I saw rodeos on the TV."

He had been on the rodeo circuit since May, but now he was going back to college, San Jose State. He was a sophomore—sort of. He said, "Since I skipped the first quarter, I'm kind of a slow sophomore. But I wanted to try it. I thought by the end of the season I would have made up my mind, but I haven't."

Dad said, "About what?"

"About school. Sophomores are supposed to choose their majors, but I haven't made up my mind about that, either."

I saw Mom glance at Danny, but Danny was focused on his chicken leg. Mom was always hoping that one of Danny's friends who went to college, like Leah Marx, for example, who had been maybe in some way and by some stretch of the imagination his girlfriend and who had gone up to Berkeley in August, would serve as a good example and lead Danny out of horseshoeing and cattle roping and into a nice safe career as an accountant.

Dad knew we were now on shaky ground and didn't say anything.

The pictures were very impressive. In fact, the pictures were a little scary. There were six of them, each one from a different rodeo, five in California and one in Nevada. Beebop was in the arena with a rider sort of on his back. He had no saddle, just the rigging that they strap where the front of a saddle would be, with a handle for the rider to hold on to, and behind that, just in front of his back legs, the other strap, which was called the flank strap. He wore a snug halter made of wide strips of leather, and he was curled in the air. Or he was stretched so that his hind hooves were pointed at the sky and his nose was nearly on the ground. His mouth was open, his ears were back, and he looked very serious and very wild.

After he laid the six photos on the kitchen table, Jerry pointed to the last one. In that one, Beebop's body was twisted and his head was down. The cowboy was flying forward, his shoulders hunched and his arms in the air. He said, "Beebop loves that move. He makes believe he's going to go forward and toss the guy, but then in the wink of an eye, he slides back and to one side and puts him over the front."

Mom glanced at the pictures and went back to washing the dishes, but Dad said, "My brother Luke liked that sort of thing. He did it for a few years when we were young. Tried bulls, too."

"I wouldn't do bulls again," said Jerry, "though I tried it for a while. And I'm not much good at bareback bronc riding—I like saddle broncs myself, but Beebop is more quick and limber than he is strong, so he's good at this. I think it's easier on him, too."

He pointed to the third picture, the one where Beebop was arched upward practically like he was going to break in two. He said, "He got the high score that time. He's good."

I said, "Do you ever ride him?"

Jerry laughed. "No way on earth. Never been on him once."

I wondered how you could have a horse and not want to ride him.

Another interesting thing about Jerry was that he talked to parents just like they were regular people. After supper, we went into the living room the way we always did, and Danny didn't leave to go home, the way he always did. The two of them sat down easy as you please. Mom picked up her knitting and everyone kept talking about this rodeo season and others gone by. It got so boring that I went to my room and read the book we were assigned in English class, which was *Spoon River Anthology*. It wasn't very long, but it was all poems, and the poems were all spoken by dead people in the cemetery. Dad would not have liked this book at all, but I thought it was spooky and interesting because it seemed like it was about people who finally got to say what they had always wanted to say after years of saying only what they were supposed to.

It was my job that night to check on the horses before bed. Rusty, our dog, was sitting on the back porch, and walked along at my side. First, I went to the geldings. It was cold enough for me to wear my jacket, so they were standing in a group under the trees, their tails facing northwest, because that was the direction the breeze was coming from. I opened the gate and went over to them. Their manes were ruffling and their coats were fluffed up. Marcus and Lincoln stayed where they were, but Blue and Jack came over, and I snaked my fingers into Blue's coat, which had a soft, warm feel. I gave everyone a couple of pieces of carrot and a scratch around the ears. Jack sniffed my pockets but wasn't pushy. I didn't mind if he was curious, just if he showed bad manners. The mares were farther away—not even visible, down in the hollow above the creek, taking shelter from the wind there. I didn't call them. I just went through the gate and looked down the hillside. Dark, quiet shapes, maybe a tail swishing back and forth in the night. Rusty stayed beside me. I knew if there was anything suspicious down there, she would take off and check it out, but she only sniffed the breeze. Then I went into the barn and looked at Beebop. He was standing quietly in his stall, having finished all of his hay. While I was looking at him, he blew air out of his nostrils, sighed, and shifted his weight. Then he flicked his ears toward me in a friendly way and made a low nicker. It was hard to believe that this was the wild horse in the pictures. I did think he needed a carrot, but I couldn't quite bring myself to hold my hand out to him, so I tossed it into his feed bin.

Even though they had gone to Danny's place the night before, and Danny's place was a twenty-minute drive, Danny and Jerry were sitting at the table when I got up for breakfast. It was barely light outside, and they were already wolfing down scrambled eggs, bacon, and toast. Danny pushed a plate toward me. I said, "Where's Mom?"

Danny said, "She's still sleeping. Jerry cooked."

I tried to pretend this was no big deal.

Jerry said, "Dan made the toast."

"That's why it's burned, then."

Danny said, "I like it that way."

Well, maybe.

The point of their coming early was that in order to introduce Beebop to Blue, Jack, Lincoln, and Marcus, we were going to set out eight piles of hay—very nice, delicious piles—and Blue, Jack, Marcus, and Lincoln would consider themselves so rich in hay that they would not mind another gelding joining them for breakfast. I couldn't help thinking of those pictures of Beebop—if he could kick that high when he was bucking a rider off, how high would he kick to show the other geldings that he was the boss? But Danny and Jerry seemed utterly relaxed. They talked about a movie that was out—*Fahrenheit 451*. Jerry had read the book. I kept eating. Danny had read the book, too. I nearly choked. I said, "What's it about?"

Jerry ate half a piece of bacon. "Well, you know, four hundred fifty-one degrees Fahrenheit is the temperature at which paper burns. It's about a future time when books are against the law, and if they find you with a book, the firemen burn it."

I turned to Danny. "You read it?"

"I liked it."

I must have looked like I didn't believe him, because he said to Jerry, "Abby doesn't think I know how to read."

I said, "What's another book you've read?"

I thought he would say something like *The Black Stallion*, but he said, "I read *A Farewell to Arms*."

16

Jerry said, "That's a good one."

I didn't believe him, though. "Why did you read that?"

"I found it on a shelf where I'm living, and there wasn't anything else to do, so I read it." He stared at me, then sniffed. "I liked it." Then he said, "You should read it."

The phone rang, and I went into the living room to get it. It was Jane, who was canceling my lessons for the day. She said, "Oh, Abby, I tried to call you last night to tell you that Melinda is down in LA for the weekend, staying with her father, and now Ellen's mom just called and said that Ellen has a hundred-and-three-degree temperature, which she only knows because Ellen started sweating and panting at the breakfast table. She's been sick for two days, but keeping it from her mother so that she could have her lesson. That girl! I've never seen anyone like her."

"I'll give her an extra one over Christmas vacation."

"I'll tell her that."

I wasn't terribly sorry not to be going to the stables. I could get my riding done and have the afternoon to myself.

Then we went out to the horses. They were hungry, since we were about half an hour late (horses always know what time it is where hay is concerned). This was part of the plan, because we wanted them to pay more attention to breakfast than to one another. Beebop knew what time it was, too—he was pawing the floor of his stall. When the four geldings were eating (and the mares, of course), Jerry got him out and took him through the gate of the gelding pasture, then led him to one of the open piles. He started to eat. Lincoln looked at him. Blue looked at him. Marcus looked at him. Jack looked at him. He did not look at them. After maybe fifteen minutes, everyone shifted piles, Lincoln first. It was Blue who moved in on Beebop's pile, but Beebop just walked over to another one and continued to eat. We watched them for half an hour, then checked on them several more times. Uneventful. When Jack came over after finishing his hay and pranced around, looking for a playmate, Beebop put his ears back. Jack paused, then trotted away, message received. Danny said, "I think they'll be okay."

Jerry said, "Beebop has no problem with other horses."

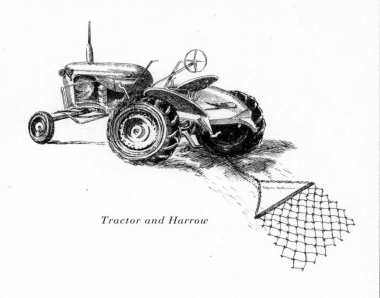

Tractor and Harrow

Wash Stall

Chapter 2

THE NEXT DAY WAS RAINY AND COLD, AND ONLY A FEW PEOPLE showed up for church—the Hollingsworths, of course, and the Brookses. Brother Abner did not show up—I couldn't remember the last time he'd stayed away. Carlie Hollingsworth and I should have been best friends. We'd known each other our whole lives, we were the same age, and we had done things together at church like babysitting and setting out and clearing up the suppers, but either she thought I was too familiar to be interesting, or I thought that of her. We didn't even try to be friends. Maybe Brother Abner was my best friend at church. He was like a grandfather or a great-uncle, but an unpredictable one, not a sour one. He sometimes told me stories of his boyhood, which had taken place in upstate New York, and had been full of adventures. The Bible passages he chose to read were usually about forgiveness and mercy. And he had a twinkle in his eye. Not many grown-ups have that. After the service, when I was making my way around the table, putting food on my plate (Sister Larkin and Sister Brooks had brought pot roast, mashed potatoes, green bean casserole, and pumpkin pie—always good), I eavesdropped as the grown-ups whispered to one another.

"Did he call you?"

"Not me. Anyone heard from him?"

Head shaking.

"You ever been to that place he has? It's only a room with a little corner for a kitchen. You can see the sky through the walls here and there. Must be freezing in this weather."

"Someone should go over there."

"He would hate that."

"Well, yes, but . . ." Glances at me, then they moved away. I took my food to my seat and picked through it. I never knew Brother Abner lived in one room with thin walls. In fact, I didn't know how most of them lived. We saw each other in church, and then it was like everyone vanished, only to reappear a few days later. I thought it was a little scary. When we were driving home, I said, "I don't remember Brother Abner ever missing a service before."

"That was worrisome," said Mom. "But look at this rain."

It was pouring, and the wipers were splashing in it.

Dad said, "I'm sure he just didn't want to drive in this. That old Studebaker he has is a little iffy. Brother Abner has seen the world and survived. He's the last one I worry about."

I said, "How old is he?"

"Oh, goodness," said Mom, "eighty-eight, maybe?"

My grandparents in Oklahoma were young enough to be his children.

"He's got a lot on the ball," said Dad. "That's for sure."

It was still raining the next day. We wore our raincoats and shuffled around the school grounds, cold and sort of miserable. It was the first real rain of the winter, and as much as we told ourselves that everywhere else in the world it was snowing, sleeting, or hailing, and the temperatures were way below zero, we were depressed. Even Stella could not use the rain to make a style statement—she wore boots and a hat and ran hunched over from class to class, just like everyone else. Sophia, however, was her usual self. We were pretty good friends now, because we always had something to talk about—horses. In history class, while Miss Cumberland was getting her slide show about Romulus and Remus organized, I told her about Vista del Canada.

She said, "They have that stallion, Encantado. There was a jumper by him, Incantation. He was nothing at the racetrack, but he could trot a five-foot jump."

"Have you ever jumped five feet?"

She shook her head very seriously. "My mom won't let me, so Jane and the colonel watch me like a hawk, but I think Onyx could do it, don't you?"

I knew enough not to encourage her, but I did think either of her horses could do it—I knew Onyx because he had once been ours, and I knew Pie in the Sky because I'd ridden him earlier in the fall. She went on, "Anyway, I would love to see Encantado." She sighed. *"Encantado* means 'delighted' or 'enchanted' in Spanish."

Miss Cumberland slapped her ruler on her desk, looked straight at us, and asked, "Do you girls have something to contribute?"

I zipped my lip, but Sophia said, "I guess that depends on the subject." She was serious. Sophia never seemed to understand sarcasm.

Because of the rain, the school bus took a long time to get to our stop, and also because of the rain, dusk seemed to be oozing over everything very early. Mom already had all the lights on, which made the house look cheerful and Christmassy. I stomped and shook myself on the front porch, to get as much rain off me as possible, but I still felt soaked when I went through the door. Rusty stood up to greet me. That meant it was really wet—Dad didn't like Rusty to come in the house, and he had said at least a hundred times that the barn was perfectly dry. Rusty of all animals knew exactly where the barn was, but sometimes Mom made up her mind, and Rusty came inside. The horses would still be out, though. Dad maintained that in spite of what we thought, they preferred it that way, and maybe they did. I planned to give them plenty of hay to help them through the night. The rain also meant no riding, though the arena had such good drainage that once the rain stopped, we could ride after about a day. The first good rain of the year disappeared especially quickly—it was as though the soil and the grass and the oaks just swallowed it down and breathed a sigh of pleasure that was the fragrance you always smelled when you opened a window or a door. I didn't mind the beginning of winter in California.

On the front table was a letter from Barbie Goldman, who was going to a very strange boarding school down near Los Angeles, where families with plenty of money paid a lot of tuition in order for their children to ride, hike, build fires, sweep, cook, argue about how the world works, and do a lot of homework. Once a week, Barbie and Alexis were driven in from "the wilds of Malibu," as Barbie called them, to a conservatory in the city, where they continued their piano and violin lessons—"our one taste of civilization," said Barbie. But the school was famous for one thing, other than roughing it, and that was art. Both twins spent a lot of time doing art. The front of this new envelope was plain white, though my name was in fancy letters, but the back had a seascape on it—a long, pale beach, a blue ocean, a few palm trees, and the white crest of a wave. I got the scissors out of Mom's sewing basket and slit it open as carefully as I could, then I cut along the sides and the bottom. After I took the envelope upstairs and tacked it to my bulletin board next to the others I'd saved, I realized that I'd almost forgotten to read the letter.

Dec. 1, 1966

Dear Abby,

The Jackson School is releasing us on our own recognizance for exactly TWO WEEKS, starting the 21st of December. Mom has agreed to allow us to come home, as long as we promise to have a party. Alexis and I have decided that a slumber party is what Mom deserves after three and a half months of peace and quiet, so prepare yourself—this is an invitation. We will have ten slumberers. I understand that you can't bring Blue, because he would have to sleep on the porch, but please sign me up for as many lessons as possible. Your mission, with regard to the slumber party, is to bring along Leslie and Sophia. DON'T TAKE NO FOR AN ANSWER. We really want to meet them. I mean, I realize that Alexis and I have known Leslie for years, but now that the butterfly is out of the chrysalis, we don't want to miss out on getting to know her better. Only three weeks until we come home— by the time you get this, it will be less. I cannot wait to sleep in a room with central heating.

You'll be surprised when you see us. We are tan and have muscles everywhere. My hair is very strange-looking. We aren't allowed to have shampoo and cream rinse— only to wash with glycerin soap, and that includes hair. So my hair has unbelievable body, but feels like twigs. As it gets colder down here, we are lucky compared to the others, though, because our instruments have to be kept in rooms with consistent temperatures. So I've never been happier to practice. I try to practice eight hours a day. We give a recital the day before we leave. It is in that room, so every single person in the school will be there, getting warm.

Mom did ask us whether we want to come back home next year and go to the high school. Alexis and I have NO idea. I think you'll have to take us on a tour of the campus so that we can decide.

Miss you,
Barbie

That was something to look forward to—a meeting between the Goldman twins and Sophia. They were like creatures from different planets.

The next day, I followed Leslie out of the lunchroom after we'd eaten, making sure first that Gloria and Stella were already on their way to their next class, which was swimming (I didn't have to take swimming until after Christmas vacation, but everyone had to pass a swimming test before the end of the year). I caught up to Leslie and we walked along for a step or two, then she glanced at me. I said, "Can I invite you to something?"

"Of course you can."

"Alexis and Barbie are coming home for Christmas and they want you to come to their slumber party. It's the twenty-first."

"I haven't been to their place since *Julius Caesar*."

I'd forgotten she'd done that with us. I said, "Who did you play?"

"Messala. Man with a torch. Woman with a torch. I don't remember saying any lines."

"You must have said something."

She smiled. "Maybe. But I don't remember."

It was on the tip of my tongue to ask what had happened to her, how she had gone from being the quiet, sort of sad and plump girl we thought we knew to this tall, self-confident, athletic girl in front of me, but I said, "I wish you'd been here for their party before they went to school. It was fun."

"I was here. But I wasn't ready to appear yet."

"Will you appear at the slumber party?"

She didn't say anything. I put my hand on her elbow. I

said, "Barbie asked me specifically to ask you and Sophia. I'm sure there will be great food and good games and . . . I don't know. There's no one like them around here now."

"Okay. It might be fun."

The next day in history, I asked Sophia. I half expected her to say, "What's a slumber party?" but instead, she said, "I've heard of the Goldmans. They used to have parts in plays. I saw them in something years ago. They're blond, right? One of them played the child in the play half the time and one of them played the child the other half. Maybe it was *Peter Pan?* Did they go to your school?"

"Yes. Now they go to the Jackson School."

"I thought of going there."

"You did?"

"Well, my dad thought of me going there. Let's put it that way. Some client of his got him all excited about it, and it took several slammed doors to talk him out of it."

I laughed.

Sophia laughed. Then she said, "Okay, I'll go to the slumber party, but maybe only as an observer."

I never knew what to make of Sophia.

A few days went by, and we didn't hear anything more from Mr. Matthews, or from Roscoe Pelham. I thought it was funny that his name was the same as the name of a type of bit. It was as if my name were "Abby Snaffle" or "Ruth Abigail Eggbutt."

On Thursday, though, the call came. Dad answered, and said, "Yes, yes. Oh, sure, that sounds fine. Let me get her," and then he handed the phone to me.

I said, "Hello?"

A smooth Southern voice said, "Is this Abby Lovitt?"

"Yes."

"Oh, Abby! Nice to be speaking to you. This is Roscoe Pelham over at Vista del Canada. I wanted to consult with you about your colt. . . . Let's see, the Jaipur colt. What's his name?"

"Jack."

"Jack?"

I said, "So far."

"Jack So Far. That's a good name. I like it. Let me write that down."

I said, "But—"

And he just kept going on, smoothly. "Well, now. I'm looking forward to meeting you. You know your brother, Daniel, has done some shoeing for us this week. He ought to work out fine, splitting his time between here and the Marble Ranch. He's a bright kid, good hand with a horse." He paused. "Jack So Far. Jack can go sooo far. Good racing handle. Jack So Far."

"Mr.—"

"Now, here's the deal. We've agreed to break the horse for Barry Matthews. He's a friend of mine, and he's got a couple of horses down there in Texas that my owner here, Mr. Leamann, wants to send to Kentucky. We normally train for the California tracks, but if they got to go east, then they got to get used to the humidity, no two ways about that. So I don't mind a little back-scratching between friends, and as we see how he goes on, well, we'll get to that, but I understand you've maintained the colt all this time, since he was born. All right, then. Daniel can just bring that young man over here, and we'll take a look at him. All right?"

"I gue—"

"Hope to meet you, too." I could hear him saying good-bye as he took the receiver of the phone away from his mouth, and then there was a click. Roscoe Pelham seemed like a nice person, but there was not going to be any getting a word in edgewise with him.

Dad had gone upstairs, and Mom had been out on the porch petting Rusty. When she came in, I said, "I guess Danny's going to take Jack over to that place."

Mom said, "I don't understand this racing business, but if . . ."

"Maybe it's just for a month or two."

"Why do you say that?"

"Well, Mr. Pelham said they would see how he gets along."

"You seem worried. What are you worried about?"

Dad came down the stairs. He said, "Putting her horse in the hands of crooks."

"Is Mr. Matthews a crook?"

"I'm not saying that."

"What are you saying, then?"

Dad shook his head, then said, "I wish I knew."

Mom laughed, and then Dad said, "It's not like we never knew any horse-racing people. We did. My mom had an uncle, back when we were kids, Uncle Bart. Uncle Bart would give you odds on whether there would be bacon for breakfast, or whether a horse who had gotten down to roll would roll all the way over. If you had a nickel, Uncle Bart would promise you a dime if two crows took off from a tree limb at the same time. If they didn't, you had to give him your nickel. He went to racetracks all over. I think he ended up in Chicago. After a while, no one ever talked about him."

"Was he saved?"

"About a hundred times," said Dad. "He liked that, too." He shook his head. "And I've seen some old racehorses, not the kind that win the Kentucky Derby and go to a nice farm for the rest of their lives, like Jaipur, but some of the ones who race twenty times a year until they're eight or nine, then go to the sale yard and can hardly walk. It's not a blessed world."

I said, "But Sophia knows a horse, a son of that stallion they have at Vista del Canada, who left the track and became a great jumper."

Mom said, "We'll take it one step at a time."

Anyway, Jaipur had won the Belmont Stakes, not the Kentucky Derby, but I didn't say anything. Had we talked about money? I thought over what Roscoe Pelham had said, and decided that what he meant was, since we'd had Jack his whole life, it was even-steven for them to give him his early training. That was enough for now.

Then Danny called that evening, and said that there was a stall opening up at Vista del Canada, because one of the two-year-olds was going to the track in San Francisco—I guess that was called Bay Meadows. So could he take Jack over the next day when he went to do some work? And then Mom said that I could take a half day off from school in order to watch him get settled. Danny said that they would keep him out in a paddock for the first week, only putting him in a stall a little bit each day for him to get used to it.

Jack hadn't been in a trailer for a month or two, not since the one time we trained him to go in with Nobby, gave him a few handfuls of oats in a bucket while he was in there, and then drove him out, just down the road and back for twenty minutes. But when Danny showed up the next morning (a sunny day!), Jack walked right into the trailer like he knew all about it, and that's what you want them to do—it shows that they figured it out. I got into the passenger's side of Danny's truck, and we set out.

With the rain and then three days of sunshine, the world we lived in was a different place—cool, bright, and breezy. Vista del Canada was in an area I had never visited—out of the way. You had to be going there to go there, and we had never had a reason to go there. All around it was a little wild—the mountains were right behind it, and the landscape wasn't open, as it was around our place. There was a locked gate—you had to press a button, and when you identified yourself, the gate swung and let you in. There was a long road that ran through a stand of trees and crossed a river. It was wild until you crested the hill, and then the place spread out before you, its own hidden valley, with paddocks and pastures and a white curving stable. The fences were not wire, either—they were board fences painted white. And the grass was thick. In California, this was a startling luxury—around our place the hills were just beginning to green up. Out by the stables, the oaks gave way to giant pines, and there were plenty of pine needles, but even the polo field wasn't very green yet. We had oaks dotting the hillsides, but here the oaks were bunched, as if this were the one spot that was rich enough and wet enough for them to gather in a forest. We passed the first stable and crested another hill. Now there stretched before us one of the most beautiful pastures I had ever seen, undulating along the side of a mountain, but not steep or rocky, just rich grass like a blanket thrown over a bed. It was divided into four parts, and several horses grazed in each one. Past the hillside, the road dipped and then turned, and went down a hill to a broad plain that ran along the river, and on this plain were three more barns and the long oval of a racetrack. One barn was quite fancy, with a small steeple and a double fence. Inside the fence, a horse was standing, looking out toward the track. Danny said, "That's the stud. His name is Encantado. He's by Stymie."

The racetrack was empty, but some more horses grazed in the center. There was grass everywhere. I said, "How do they keep it so green?"

"They irrigate, silly."

"How can they afford that? Mr. Jordan doesn't do that." The Jordan Ranch was the biggest ranch in our neighborhood, and Mr. Jordan had plenty of money.

"Well, he isn't by the river, for one thing, and he doesn't own lots of banks, for another."

"What's on that hillside?"

"That's a vineyard. They also grow grapes, olives, and almonds."

The racetrack drew my eye, even though there was no one on it. Between the two green fields, the one in the middle and the one around it, was a silver oval, level, with tiny, even, lengthwise lines. Next to the gate at one end was a large green tractor with a harrow attached to it. They must groom the track every day.

No doubt there were bigger farms in Kentucky, but this farm was nestled so perfectly and beautifully in the mountains that you could not stop looking around. Next to every beautiful thing that there was to look at was another beautiful thing to look at, if only an oak tree surrounded by a hedge, or rosebushes climbing over a fence, or the dark hillside rising from the green meadow. The oaks were streaming with moss, and because of the mountains, the sky was more like a perfect backdrop to the picture than real, hard sky. Maybe it rained and stormed here, but it looked like paradise.

The barns were two rows of stalls. All the stalls opened onto a neatly groomed gravel path that was shaded by an overhang. There were pots of geraniums at the corners of the overhang. In the V formed by the two barns, there was a circular track with footing like the racetrack's, where the horses could be walked by grooms. This track was surrounded by a thick hedge, maybe three feet high and two feet wide, with three entrances—one facing the racetrack and one facing each of the barns. There was a flower bed just below the hedge with marigolds blooming. The horses looked out over their half doors, or they could go to the back of their stalls and step out into individual runs. This meant that they basically had two stalls—one inside and one outside. If it was raining, the door to the outside could be closed. Everything was very neat, and looked like perfect luxury to me—most stables you see, no matter how fancy, look at least a little run-down from horses breaking the fences or kicking their stalls or just making a mess, but not Vista del Canada.

A man was waiting beside the barns. He stepped up to my side of the truck as soon as we stopped. I rolled down my window, and he put his hand in and said, "Well, you must be Abby Lovitt. A pleasure to meet you, ma'am. I am Roscoe Pelham, you may call me Ross. Beautiful day today, horses were out a little later than they are in the summer, we don't have a lighted track, not like down south, where they get 'em out by five, no matter what time of the year it is. So, let's see this young fella. Anyway, glad you could bring him over on such short notice—we don't like an empty stall. Makes everyone lazy."

I said, "Hi."

Jack had been good all the way over—no rocking, no getting his foot caught, no blood anywhere, *and* no sweat when we backed him down the ramp. His coat was as smooth and dry as when I brushed him that morning.

Once down the ramp, he lifted his head and his tail, pricked his ears, gave a loud, sharp whinny. Six horses answered him back, including Encantado, which made Jack snort and prance a couple of steps in place. He didn't act scared—he acted ready to take over.

Ross said, "Self-confident young fella, and big for his age. What's his birth date?"

"January twenty-second."

"Very good. Very good. As old as he can be. You know, there was a time when the official birth date for Thorough-breds was May first, rather than January first. Could be it was better that way." He smiled. "You'd be surprised how it is in Kentucky. Some of those newborn foals come out of their stalls on the second of January quite muscular and active." He laughed. Danny led Jack over to an empty paddock and put him in there, carefully turning him and taking off his halter. Jack reared up and twisted away, then did a high-stepping trot to the other side of the paddock. He stopped there for a moment of stillness, then he leapt, kicked up, and galloped back toward the gate, twisting and turning just as he got there, and then running to the right in a big circle. He was only a year-ling, but he wasn't going to tell them that. I said, "Will he be okay?"

Mr. Pelham said, "He moves like a cat. He's not going to get himself in trouble, and there's no one in there with him to get him into trouble. I'll watch him."

Danny nodded, then said, "I can come over every day."

This was reassuring. I didn't see how I would have left Jack there if Danny had not started his new job, partly shoe-ing and partly working with young horses. Lucky again.

I said, "My friend was telling me about Incantation."

"Oh, he was slow. He only had three starts. If there was something worse than last place, he would have found it. But he's good-looking. Looks like his pop. He found himself a niche as a jumper; not all of them do."

We walked over toward the track and the stallion pen. Encantado had gone inside, but when Mr. Pelham gave a whistle, he emerged. Mr. Pelham said, "We have to admire him from a distance. He bites a lot even for a stud. But he could jump out of that paddock if he only realized it."

The fence was at least five feet high.

Mr. Pelham said, "Course, studs are a little more chicken about jumping than geldings."

Encantado whinnied. His whinny made Jack's whinny sound puny and childish. Then his tail went up and he arched his neck and sprang in a very bright trot along the length of the fence, bringing each of his four feet high off the ground, as if he were trotting on hot coals. He snorted.

Danny said, "He has a very good opinion of himself."

"Well, he won the Hollywood Gold Cup and the Santa Anita Handicap, so he would. What's your Jaipur colt's name again?"

I said, "Jack So Far."

Danny glanced at me.

"Oh, yes. You told me that. Nice one. Warn Matthews told me how you got him. Amazing story."

I said, "I never know whether it makes me feel unbelievably lucky or unbelievably sad."

"I know what you mean," said Roscoe Pelham. "Well, I got a bit of work to do, but here's Ike. He'll answer any questions you have. Very pleased to meet you." He shook my hand again, then strode across the grass to his truck, pausing to give Encantado the once-over (Encantado pinned his ears and snaked his nose toward the fence; Ross laughed). You could tell he was the boss by the way his eyes moved here and there, focusing on this cracked fence rail or that piece of machinery not parked properly. Things to be fixed.

Just then, a man walked out of one of the barns with some

bridles in his hand. He hung them on a hook at the corner of the barn, then waved to us. Danny said, "That's Ike. He's the head groom."

Ike trotted over, his hand out for a handshake. Danny remembered his manners. They smiled and chatted for a minute, then Ike said something, and Danny nodded, and they smiled again, and Ike shook his head. Then Danny gestured toward the car, and Ike came around to my side. My window was down, so Ike stuck his hand in for me to shake it. He said, "Well, now, hello there, Abby. I'm Ike. Pleased t' meet ya. How are ya t'day?"

"I'm fine, thank you."

"Now, I hear ya own yerself that yearlin'?"

I nodded.

"That's startin' young, I'll say that for ya. Ya mighta waited till ya had some sense, but what fun is that?"

I didn't know what to make of this.

"Well, he's a good-lookin' youngster. Not a speck of white on 'im."

I said, "He has three white hairs for a star."

Ike laughed. "Well, miss, maybe that's good luck. We'll see. He's got long legs and he's got muscle, though. That's the best combination. I'll say one thing, they live like sultans here. They want somethin', they just ring the bell and we come runnin'!" He laughed.

Danny laughed.

I laughed.

I handed him the list I'd written out, of what Jack was used to eating, and what vaccinations he had had and when.

Danny was the person who trimmed his feet, so that wouldn't be a problem. I said, "I guess I should have brought some carrots."

Ike laughed. He said, "You want carrots? We got carrots. Mr. Pelham is a great believer in carrots."

Somehow, that was what made me feel like maybe this was the best place for Jack after all.

Ike waved and went to his bridles. Danny and I drove around the smaller barn and headed back past the racetrack. There was a nice breeze wafting up the river, and you could see it kind of sparkling on the other side of the trees. Then we passed Encantado again, who gave a lonesome whinny, and we went back up the hill. From this angle, you could also see the house, which was nestled in the trees to the left. It was very large, a creamy white with a bright red tile roof and a veranda that ran along the front. The way it was set, the people in the house could look out over the horses in the pastures. As we drove by the pastures, we could see that the horses were being led back to yet another big barn. The paddocks beside the curved front barn were empty, too. I guess they were buttoning things up for the day. I said, "What time is it?"

"'Bout three-fifteen."

"They go to bed early here."

"Well, I guess they keep a racetrack schedule, to get the horses used to it."

"Horses don't mind getting up early."

"We only ever had one that slept in. You remember Papa George?"

I shook my head. Once upon a time, Dad had named all

the geldings "George" and all the mares "Jewel." So if the name was George, I didn't remember many of them at all.

"He slept until you threw out the hay. Palomino, he was. The other horses would be milling around, and he'd just be stretched out on his side. And then Dad would toss the hay over the fence, and he'd get up and yawn a couple of times, then go to the open flake and start eating. Makes me yawn just to think about it."

We went up the road between the trees and the gate opened and closed behind us. I said, "Looks expensive."

Danny nodded.

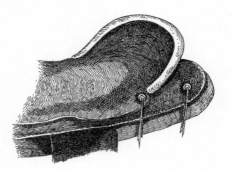

Saddle Cantle

English Girth

Chapter 3

THE NEXT MORNING WAS BRIGHT AGAIN, AND EVEN WHAT YOU might call warm. Melinda was still in Los Angeles, but Ellen was fully recovered and ready for her lesson. Even her pigtails were extra bouncy. As soon as Mom pulled into the parking lot, Ellen ran to the car and said, "You're late!"

Her mother, who was a few steps behind her, said, "Ellen! Say hello!"

"Hello! You're late!"

I said, "I guess we should get started, then." I got out of the car.

Her mother breathed a deep sigh. I could see Mom sort of laughing. She waved, backed up, and drove off to buy groceries. Ellen ran ahead of me to the barn, and by the time I got there, the groom, Rodney, had set her on Gallant Man, the pony, and she was ready to go. I said, "Ellen, you're getting pretty big."

"I'm not the shortest girl in my class anymore. Beverley Morton is half an inch shorter. And Petey King is shorter than I am, too, but that's because he skipped a grade."

"Since you're growing, it's time you learned to mount from the ground. Even if you don't do it as a rule, you should be able to, from the right and from the left, in case you are ever out on a trail or something and you have to get on."

"I can do that."

"Okay, do it."

Her chin pushed out. She said, "Right now?"

"Right now."

By this time, her mother was nearby and watching. Out of the corner of my eye, I saw her get a little nervous.

There was a pause. Were we heading for a tantrum?

I said, "First, you learn the traditional way, then maybe you can learn some tricks."

She relaxed, stood up in her stirrups, brought her right leg over his haunches, and scrambled to the ground. Gallant Man stood like a rock. I said, "We'll work on that, too."

Then I said, "Pat your pony."

Ellen stroked Gallant Man's neck several times, and by the fifth or sixth time, I saw that she was more relaxed. I also saw that her eyebrows came just about to the pony's withers, so since he was over twelve hands, that meant she was about four foot four. It might be a little hard for her, but Ellen was always up for a challenge.

First things first. I said, "Make sure your girth is tight."

She slipped her fingers between the girth and the pony. Easily. I said, "There was a girl at the show last summer who forgot to tighten her girth, and when she mounted, the saddle just slid all the way to the side. Her pony jumped away, and she could have gotten hurt." Ellen gave me a serious look, then pulled the straps, with some effort, up one hole. I checked it to make sure it was tight enough, and then she checked it. I guess it was then that I realized that Ellen, for all of her enthusiasm, had never been asked to do any of the work. Rodney did it for her.

I showed her how to stand facing the pony, how to take the reins in her left hand and lift her foot and set it firmly in the stirrup, how to make sure her pony was square on all four feet, how to give herself a little spring and catch the mane and the cantle of the saddle in her hands, launch herself, then throw her right leg over the pony's haunches and lower herself into the seat of the saddle—never bounce or drop. She had good spring and she was only a little awkward, but she was not satisfied. She dismounted and tried two more times. Each time was better. After the third time, she said, "That was good." And it was. Part of Ellen's charm (and some people would be surprised to learn that she had any) was that she always knew when she had done something properly. As we walked to the ring, she said, "What are some tricks?"

"Well, Indian-style is jumping on over his tail. Or you can get a running start from the front, grab his mane with your left hand, and vault on from the side. Or you can get a running start from the back and sort of throw yourself up. I think that's the hardest, probably." I had tried the second way, but neither of the other ways.

As we entered the arena, Ellen said, "I want to do all of those."

Of course she did.

Her mother didn't follow us—she knew better. We had a good lesson: lots of circles and transitions, both between gaits and from slow to fast and fast to slow within gaits. She went through the cavalletti five or six times, then I set up her favorite jumping exercise, which was three jumps in a long row, end to end, that she could approach from either side. First, she trotted them a few times in a figure eight, with the middle jump the pivot. She had done this in lessons twice before. This time, I let her canter them. After the second jump each way, she had to ask Gallant Man to shift his balance, move over, and take the other lead. She was systematic and careful about it, and she got her changes in both directions. Once, when he went from his not-so-good lead to his good lead, he made a flying change. I said, "Did you feel that?"

Ellen said, "Yes."

"That was a flying change."

She said, "It felt like ballet."

When her mom came to meet us after the lesson, I had Ellen dismount, mount again, and dismount. I said, "She's getting good."

Her mother said, "Oh, wonderful!" but she didn't look very happy. I decided that riding was more of a challenge for Ellen's mom than it was for Ellen.

* * *

46

Ever since our Ralph Carmichael clinic, I'd tried once a week to give Blue a jumping lesson that was pure fun. The arena was now dry after the rain, so I went out after lunch and started moving poles. Blue wandered around the arena while I was doing this—I wanted him to know what was coming, and to look forward to it, and maybe he did. He'd lost his fear of jumping, as far as I could tell. Had I lost mine? That, I couldn't tell. Before our problems with jumping in the early fall, I wouldn't have said that I was afraid, but I also thought that when Black George, now Onyx, was my jumper, I didn't know enough to be afraid. Onyx jumped for the love of it. You didn't even have to steer him all that well; you just had to point him in the general direction of a fence and he would go there on his own. A jump had to be pretty big not to seem small if Onyx was under you. When I was riding Sophia's other horse, Pie in the Sky, I was not afraid, either, or at least, not afraid of the jumping. I was more afraid of the sense I had with him that having his own way was more important to him than being safe or doing it properly. He didn't seem trustworthy—it seemed as though if he felt he had to pick a fight with you, he would pick one, no matter where you were on the course. I had seen fancy jumpers at horse shows do just that with their riders.

As for Blue, well, it got to the point where it didn't matter who was afraid, him or me. His fear made me feel like I had no idea what I was doing, and I suppose that my fear made him feel also like I didn't know what I was doing, and so, who was in charge, really? But these little fun lessons helped us both. He could jump around here and there and learn how to use his body, and whether I knew what I was doing was unimportant. Today, I set up a three-stride along the fence, 2'6", two simple jumps with sixteen of my big steps between them—four for every stride and one for the takeoff. Then I set a line of poles about three feet high along the inner edge of the two fences, opposite the rail. This was the chute. Blue now quite liked the chute, so at the beginning, I only had to set one pole to guide him in. I wanted him to go through the chute both directions, so I put one of these poles at each end.

It took a while to set up the chute. The whole time, Blue was walking around and trotting around. Once, he whinnied to the other horses, and one of the mares answered him. When that happened, he cantered for a few strides—even Blue could be a show-off with the proper incentive. After I was finished building the chute, I followed him for a minute or two with the whip in my hand, just to get him to play a little more. When I put the whip down and turned away, he came trotting in my direction. I caught him, attached the lead rope to his halter, and did his Jem Jarrow exercises—stepping over at the walk, stepping over at the trot, backing up, repeating this on both sides—until I felt that he was soft and relaxed. He wasn't as good as Jack at the hardest exercise, which was to be trotting in a tight circle, feel me tug on the lead rope and turn, still trotting, and go the other direction—but he was good enough. I unclipped the lead rope and led him to the end of the chute. I showed him a carrot, then ran to the other end of the chute. He didn't follow me, since I had run around the jumps, but he stood there with his ears pricked, and when I called him, he trotted down over the jumps, came to me, and took his carrot.

I ran to the other end. He trotted back the other way, and took his carrot.

Now was the time that I wished I had a friend like Daphne or Andy Carmichael at the far end, so I wouldn't have to run back and forth, but Blue was patient, and did it twice in each direction. Then I did what the Carmichaels also did, which was to tack up, get on, and do the exact same thing you had been doing, only mounted. Blue was good. I didn't go on to the next step, like Daphne, which was to take off the bridle and go down over the jumps with my arms in the air. Danny and I agreed that we'd never met anyone like Daphne. Even Andy wasn't like Daphne.

Once I'd cooled Blue and put him away, then taken Oh My on a trail, ponying Nobby, it was getting late and I was tired, but all the horses were exercised—Dad had done Marcus, Lincoln, and Lady in the morning (he was talking about borrowing a couple of calves from Mr. Jordan to give Lady some practice at cutting), and it didn't look like Beebop was expected to do anything but enjoy his vacation. I paused to watch him when I passed out the hay. He and Lincoln were now a pair, and Blue had taken up with Marcus, though this did not seem to be a close friendship—there was a little bit of ear pinning and an occasional raised hoof. No doubt Blue felt that he, as the older horse, should always be giving the orders, and no doubt Marcus felt that he, as a world-class beauty whose entire family was famous, should not be taking orders from a mere Thoroughbred. However, they did not look as though they were really going to argue. I was sure all of the geldings were glad that Jack the Pest was gone. And now it was dark.

I took my boots off on the back porch and went in yawning. Something smelled good, and I hoped Mom was making meat loaf. The first person I saw as I opened the back door was Danny, and the second was Jerry Gardino. Jerry had an apron on and a spatula in his hand. Danny was holding a kitchen knife. I said, "What are you making?"

Jerry said, "Cannelloni."

I could not imagine what this was. Danny started chopping an onion. I decided I had no idea what was going on, and walked on into the living room. Mom was sewing two pieces of her afghan together and Dad was looking at some papers. I kept going.

It turned out that cannelloni was very large noodles—rather like the egg noodles that Mom sometimes made, but as wide as your hand—rolled around some sort of white cheese and then covered with a spaghetti sauce, topped with more cheese, and baked in the oven. It was exactly the sort of thing you would have at the Goldmans' house, and you would taste it politely a few times until you decided that it was pretty good and there was nothing else and you might as well eat it. Danny and Jerry each had two helpings; Dad, after a slow start, had a helping and a half, and Mom was polite. I pushed the white part to one side; the rest was good, and I ate it. It was true that Danny would eat anything, had always been ready to eat anything, including asparagus, which Mom grew behind the house and only made us eat in the spring, when it was very young. If you put enough brown butter on it, it was fine. There was also salad. I ate that. I thought that this must be what Sophia felt like most of the time—it was on her plate, staring at her, she knew she ought to eat it, but in the end, why bother?

In the meantime, Dad was quizzing Jerry about his family, as if they had come from Mars or something. When he asked what his grandfathers did, Danny and I just kept our eyes on our plates (Jerry's grandfathers were both butchers), but when he asked where the family went to church, we glanced at each other. Danny's left eyebrow, the one toward me, lifted slightly. I coughed. Jerry laughed and said, "They all go to Saints Peter and Paul. It's a pretty famous church. It was bombed five times in the twenties, and then Joe DiMaggio got married there, though not to Marilyn Monroe. To his first wife. My mom saw the celebration when she was a kid." He spoke cheerfully. It was clear that Danny had not said a word to Jerry about Dad or Mom or our church. Jerry thought he was just conversing.

Dad said, "I never heard of that church. But I guess, even though I've been up around there, I've never actually been in the city of San Francisco."

Now it was Jerry's turn to have his jaw drop to his plate. He said, "You've never crossed the Golden Gate Bridge? You've never been to Chinatown or the Embarcadero?"

And Dad said, "Maybe we should go there sometime."

Danny said, "You should."

That was how we knew that Danny had been there without ever telling us. I was sure he'd been up to visit Leah Marx.

Mom said, "I hear that people like to walk across the Golden Gate Bridge."

"It's a beauty," said Jerry. "I've done that twice. If there's a high wind, it trembles. But they don't allow you to walk across it in certain weather conditions."

Dad said, "Hmph. So your family are Roman Catholic."

Jerry said, "Most Italians are. I was an altar boy for six years." He continued to eat, now his salad. I could see that Dad was toying with whether he should witness to Jerry. A Catholic was unsaved, according to our church, and it was his job to witness to everyone who was unsaved. All we knew about Catholics was that they bowed down to statues of saints and they worshiped Jesus on the cross—not Jesus himself, but an image of him. Also, Catholics could only talk to Jesus through Mary or the Pope. I started holding my breath. Maybe Mom started holding her breath—she was poking at her salad with her fork. But Dad, I guess, decided not to risk it. Jerry was Danny's friend. Danny and Dad had gone months and months without speaking, and things had only gotten more or less (sometimes less) back to normal in the summer. I could hear all of Danny's arguments in my head, too—he is our guest, he didn't ask you, his religion is not our business (your business). I could even see them as I had so many times in the past, looking alike as they sat across from one another at the kitchen table, slamming their coffee cups down just before jumping up and not speaking to one another for another month. There was a silence—not long enough for Jerry to notice—and then Mom said, "What's for dessert?"

"Oh!" said Jerry. "I got something at a bakery in San Jose. It's in a box in the truck." He pushed away from the table and went out the back door. I started clearing the plates. The long silence continued. I wasn't quite sure whether or not the danger had passed. Then Jerry came in, and he was carrying a box of large round cookies with ridges in fancy shapes. He said, "These are pizzelle. The bakeries only have them around Christmas and Easter. I love them. They aren't terribly sweet." He set the box on the table, and we each took one. They were crisp and tasted like black licorice.

Mom said, "You like to cook."

"I love to cook. That's my hobby. But at my house, I can hardly get to the stove, because everyone else is there first, arguing about what to have for dinner. So this is fun for me. And there isn't a real kitchen in my dorm at school, just a hot plate." Then he said, "I had my apprentice meat cutter's license when I was sixteen. Youngest in our family. But I don't know. There are other things to do in life besides cooking and eating."

Maybe there had never been anyone like Jerry Gardino in our house. He was good-natured and a little loud, and he moved around a lot. He leaned from side to side in his chair; he waved his hands and even his arms. He smiled. His hair bounced. While he was eating (he was sitting beside me), he tapped his foot. He turned his chair away from the table, stretched his legs, crossed them at the ankles. I looked over at the stove—he did not believe in "clean as you go." I guess I'd thought that Beebop would be wild in the pasture, but it turned out that Beebop was quiet in the pasture but Jerry was wild in the house.

Even so, Mom and Dad seemed to like him. When he and Danny left that evening (after cleaning up, of course, though I helped), Mom said, "Come back anytime," just the way Mrs. Goldman said it, as if she actually meant it.

* * *

53

Since the next day was beautiful, everyone was at church. What with all of the events of the week, I had forgotten about Brother Abner. He was missing again. Apparently, Sister Hazen and Sister Larkin had decided to go see him. Before the hymns started, I heard them talking to Mom about it. Sister Hazen said, "I'd been there before, about fifteen months ago. I went there to deliver a chair we gave him, and I have to say the place looked a little basic then, but . . ."

"You know he uses an outhouse," said Sister Larkin. "Just like the old days. I grew up with an outhouse." She clucked and waved her hand.

"And if he wants hot water, he heats it on his range. He said to me he thought piped-in hot water was bad for you. Lead in the pipes."

"A bath a week, according to him, Saturday night, and he uses one piece of soap. Carries it from one sink to the other, until it's down to a little bead."

"That's very frugal," said Mom.

"Oh, 'frugal' isn't the word," said Sister Hazen.

Sister Larkin said, "But those are the old ways. Go to bed at dusk, read the same few books over and over, use up your bar of soap. When my folks got electric light on the farm, my mother was ashamed of how dirty the walls were, but that was decades of gas lamps and kerosene lamps for you."

Mom said, "But does he seem ill?"

"Oh, he does," said Sister Larkin. "Coughing into his handkerchief, then asking us if we'd like a cup of tea. My land! I am worried."

Mom said, "Was his place cold?"

"Well, it was a sunny day, and his place faces south. It was warm enough that afternoon, but it must get chilly. Must. The little woodstove looked unused to me, though there was some firewood in the kindling box. Maybe he doesn't feel good enough to put a fire in there, and he thinks that blankets will be enough."

"He's very thin," said Mom.

"Gracious me, I was shocked!" said Sister Larkin, who loved to cook and looked it.

Then they all started shaking their heads.

Sister Hazen said, "He thanked us for coming, but with these old men, you never know what to do. Pride means everything to them, and they don't want anyone to see how they are. I sometimes think . . ." She shook her head again, then said, "Well, what is the charitable thing to do? Hurt their pride by saving them, or let them go on the way they want to?"

Sister Larkin said, "And you can't ask them, because they won't give you a straight answer." All three women started tutting.

After that, we had our usual service, with five hymns before the brothers started sharing the passages in the Bible that they wanted to talk about, then some more hymns, which were my favorite part, because Dad had a good voice and Mom knew how to harmonize. After that, supper, which Sister Lodge and Sister Larrabee had made, chicken stew and boiled potatoes, with cupcakes for dessert. But I could see the talk about Brother Abner go around the room. Two or three people would lean toward one another, heads would bend, lips would move, heads would shake, then those people would talk to someone else. The sisters would talk to each other, then to their own male relatives, then the men would talk to each other. It would be Dad and Mr. Hollingsworth and Mr. Brooks who would be expected to come up with an idea. I didn't know what it would be, though.

At the end of the meal, there was plenty of chicken left, some potatoes, and two cupcakes. Sister Lodge said that she would take the food by Brother Abner's place and tell him the congregation was thinking of him. Everyone agreed that that was not only a charitable thing to do, but a tactful one. On the way home, Mom and Dad mumbled in the front seat. I could have leaned forward and heard them, but I didn't. I had no ideas, either.

It may be that Kyle Gonzalez had seen every movie about the Roman Empire ever made, or at least he had read about them. Whenever Miss Cumberland said any name at all—Antony, Caesar, Cleopatra, Marcus Aurelius, Scipio, Carthage—Kyle would raise his hand and ask if she had seen the movie about that person. His favorites were *Ben-Hur, Spartacus,* and something about Hannibal, which was in Italian, which Kyle did not know, but he enjoyed the film anyway. I supposed that he was allowed to stay up all night, anytime he wanted, and watch old movies on TV. All I knew before we studied the Romans in class was the Bible stories and the Shakespeare play *Julius Caesar,* which we had read at the end of seventh grade. I was very fond of that play because we did a reading of it at the Goldmans' house, and that was when I started to be friends with them. Since we had spent a little too much time on the Greeks, Miss Cumberland's favorite, we had to rush through the last four hundred years of the Roman Empire before we took our test on Friday. In the spring, we were to go on to medieval Europe.

My favorite thing about the Roman Empire was that it got as far as England, which Miss Cumberland said was as far away from Rome as we were from Colorado Springs, which might not seem very far, but try walking, which is what the Roman soldiers had to do. Miss Cumberland was very fond of Hadrian, who was one of the good emperors and who visited England and built a wall there that still stands. He also visited Egypt and Jerusalem. He liked to take architects with him and have buildings and temples built. She showed us a slide show of some of the buildings, as well as of statues of Hadrian, and she also said that a French writer had written a book called *Memoirs of Hadrian*. I was sure Kyle would do an extra-credit report on it by Friday. We were looking forward to Christmas vacation. Once the tests were over Friday, we would have eighteen days. I did not expect to do well on my test, but thanks to being friends with Sophia, who didn't mind explaining things, I had gotten an A on the Egyptians, an A-minus on the Sumerians, a B-plus on the early Greeks, and an A on the classical Greeks. These grades averaged out to an A-minus, so a C on the Romans would only take me down to a B-plus for the whole semester. A B-plus would get past Dad, no problem. However, the week was hard work, with scads of homework, more than I could do on the way home on the bus. Mom helped me by always riding Nobby and Lincoln. Dad rode Oh

My and Marcus, and I let Blue slide a little. I would catch up in the course of eighteen days of vacation.

About the only fun at school for that whole week was lunch, and even then, we spent a lot of time listening to Sophia explain geometry problems to Stella, who listened carefully, but always seemed amazed at what she heard. At least, she was no longer getting an F or even a D—thanks to Sophia, she was getting a C-plus. I liked geometry. I thought it was pretty easy to picture what the teacher was talking about, and as for the numbers, you just had to memorize them. Even pi you only had to memorize out to four decimal places—3.1415. It was like a good phone number—3+1=4+1=5. Sophia's phone number was like that, 835-1448: 8−3=5−1=4+4=8. I didn't tell anyone that that was how I memorized stuff. I thought it sounded too much like Kyle Gonzalez.

The other interesting thing at school was that Leslie had a boyfriend, and he was a Condor. True, he was a basketball Condor (and taller than she was) rather than a football Condor (the basketball team had had a 6–3 season, and so they were pretty popular). He was a junior. His name was Ronny Wood, and sometimes he sat with us at lunch. Leslie always sat with us. She said that if he wanted to have lunch with her, he had to sit with us, too. He was a guard on the basketball team, and as a sophomore had averaged fifteen points a game. Leslie said that this was good. He had a driver's license, and he brought her to school every morning by seven o'clock. They ran at least two miles around the track before changing and going to class.

All in all, I liked high school better than I thought I was going to, but there was a lot to think about. You couldn't just roll out of bed and put some clothes on and go, making sure you were clean and your hair was combed. You had to have made up your mind about all sorts of things, like what group you wanted to look like (even though you might not be a part of that group), whether you wanted to stick out or fade into the woodwork (I wanted to fade into the woodwork), whether you wanted the teachers to like you, *really* like you, or just get along with you. The high school was big, and there were a lot of ways to be famous there, not all of them good. Stella and Gloria said that you had to *seize* your opportunity, and talked a lot about what opportunities there were. So there were plenty of reasons I was glad to see the end of the semester. No one in my family had had to worry about any of this—Mom and Dad had gone to a country school in Oklahoma that had about ten students of all ages, and Danny had quit (after goofing off most of the time before that).

Braided Rope Reins

Racing Bridle

Chapter 4

THURSDAY NIGHT, JUST BEFORE DINNER, DANNY ROLLED UP TO the gate in his truck, pulling a strange trailer—not Jake Morrisson's and not Jerry Gardino's. He honked, and since I was on the front porch, not having yet taken off my boots, I ran out and opened the gate. It was nearly dark. He pulled through, then I closed the gate, latched it, and ran after the truck and trailer to the barn. Dad was out haying the horses. Dad never stopped what he was doing in order to do something else—he said that "one thing at a time" was the key to success—but nevertheless, he did walk fast to the barn when he had thrown out the last flakes, pushing the wheelbarrow ahead of him.

By that time, Danny had the ramp of the trailer down and

the horse unfastened up front. He unhooked the tail chain, and the horse backed down the ramp, one step at a time. He was almost pure white, with only a few dapples around his knees. And he was huge, bigger than Dad's favorite horse, Lester, that he'd sold to Mr. Jordan, bigger than Onyx, bigger than Pie in the Sky. At the bottom of the trailer, he lifted his head and flared his nostrils. He stood absolutely still. He was so white he seemed to shine in the dusk. Danny said, "Meet Gee Whiz." Then he added, "By Hyperion, out of Tilla, by Birkhahn."

The back door opened, and Mom came out with a wooden spoon in her hand. There was a whinny from the mares, and then there was a whinny from the geldings. Gee Whiz pawed once, flared his nostrils, and answered. He was loud, no doubt because he had a huge chest. I said, "Is that horse over seventeen hands?"

"Seventeen-one," said Danny.

Seventeen hands and one inch is big for a horse—and I could see that his withers were above the brim of Danny's hat.

"What in the world would you do with such a big horse?" said Dad.

"Well, he's been a racehorse his whole life. He's eight, he's had sixty starts, he's won a hundred thirty-four thousand dollars, and he's finished. Mr. Pelham will think of something to do with him, but they are full up for now, so I said we could put him up for a month, seventy-five dollars, until some of the two-year-olds go to the track and open up some space. As far as I can tell, he's sound as can be." Danny turned him in a little circle, then took him into the barn, where he put him into a stall. That seventy-five dollars was another little reason not to sell Oh My too quickly, or to find a place for Lady before she really knew what to do with a calf. Marcus, Beebop, and Gee Whiz. Looked like we were in the boarding business.

Danny was excited, which was unusual, because Danny was like Dad—he thought getting excited was a pretty sure way to get disappointed. About the most Danny or Dad ever did was hope for the best. But after Danny cleaned out the trailer and turned it around, then came in for supper, he was smiling and bouncy. I was setting the table. I said, "You didn't buy yourself a horse, did you?"

Danny laughed. He said, "I *have* a horse. No, I just . . . I don't know. There's something about this guy, the way he's been around, done his job. I mean, he's a beauty."

"He's a giant," said Dad. "I'm surprised he's still sound."

"Yes," said Danny as we sat down, "but look at his bone. He must have nine inches of bone."

This was, basically, the circumference of his foreleg below the knee. The more the better.

All through dinner, Danny babbled on and on about Gee Whiz. It was like he had never seen a racehorse before, and maybe he hadn't. I couldn't think of any racehorses we knew. But he was working at Vista del Canada now, and they had won him over.

Did we know who Hyperion was?

Of course not.

Well, Hyperion was an English racehorse, born in 1930. In thirteen starts, he had nine wins, one second, and two thirds. Two of his wins were English races like the Kentucky

Derby and the Belmont Stakes. And he was maybe the greatest sire of the twentieth century, with winning offspring all over the world, in Australia and France, and everywhere. Had we heard of Pensive?

Mom said, "That's a nice name."

"Pensive won the Derby and the Preakness, and almost the Triple Crown—he was second in the Belmont Stakes. *And* he sired Ponder, who won the Kentucky Derby, and was the sire of Needles. Needles won the Derby in 1956."

Dad said, "I do remember Needles. He was a good horse."

"Well, he was named Needles because he got pneumonia as a foal, and they had to give him so many shots, that's what they named him, but he was a great horse. In the Derby, he came from fifteenth out of sixteen, and in the Belmont Stakes, he came from behind to win again. Anyway, this horse, Gee Whiz, is from Hyperion's last crop, and he is related to all of those other great horses. Of course, he got his size from the dam's side, because Hyperion was tiny, maybe the size of Oh My." Danny took a deep breath and actually started eating his food. I hadn't seen many things that prevented Danny from diving into a minute steak with baked potatoes and gravy, but imagining all of Gee Whiz's relatives had done the trick.

I knew how he felt. When Warn Matthews had sent me Jack's probable pedigree (*if* he was the real son of Jaipur and Alabama Lady, and these days everyone said that he was), I had memorized the names of the horses and said them in my head every night for a while as I was going to sleep. The names were like little fairy tales all in a word or a phrase: Rare Perfume, Sir Gallahad, Blenheim, Nasrullah, Scapa Flow,

Priam, Asterus, Mahmoud. I thought for a moment, then said, "I need to get something."

I ran up the stairs and went into my room. The pedigree was neatly folded in the top right-hand drawer. I grabbed it and ran down the stairs. When I put it on the table, there it was, Jack's great-grandsire on his dam's side was Hyperion, through a horse called Alibhai, who was born in 1938. And his son, Determine, had also won the Kentucky Derby. That was Jack's grandsire. So Jack and Gee Whiz were related.

Danny said, "It's like Gee Whiz is his great-granduncle."

Dad said, "Believe me, there are lots and lots of cousins, and very few of them have done much."

But still, it was interesting to think about.

After supper, Danny and I went out to have another look at Gee Whiz. I admit I was more drawn to him now that I knew he was related to Jack. I saw more grace in his movement and more intelligence in his eye. But he was, indeed, a striking horse, and only part of that was how big he was (good thing the stalls in our barn were really big, much bigger than the stalls out at the stables, which was part of the reason we hardly ever kept a horse in them—most horses take the opportunity to poop all over a big stall, so cleaning a big stall is more work, and bedding a big stall takes more straw). He was tall but he was graceful—as we stood there looking at him, he curved around the stall, and his strides were big but precise. At the same time, he kept his eye on us, not as if he was suspicious, but as if he was curious. He put his head over the door. I had some carrots in my pocket, and Danny had two cubes of sugar. He took them politely. Then, after I asked Danny when he had last raced, and just as Danny said, "He raced Sunday," Gee Whiz lifted his nose and, very gently, sniffed my hair and then my shoulder. I'd never had a horse do that before. I stood still. Danny didn't stop him or reprimand him, as Dad might have done. Danny had learned from Jem Jarrow that a horse can be curious, and that that is a good thing. A curious horse is intelligent.

When Gee Whiz went back to his hay, Danny said, "He ran at Hollywood Park Sunday, in the last race, and I guess he was the oldest horse in the race, and he ran fifth out of ten. The trainer called Mr. Leamann and said that he ran a game race, but he had done his work, and it was time to do something else. I guess he came back to the barn a little depressed."

"Do you think that's true? That a horse knows he got beaten and feels sad?"

Danny said, "Why not? If he knows what racing is about, then he knows what winning is about, and he can't be good at it without wanting to win. If he wants to win, then he knows if he's lost."

I said, "What about the carrot? What about the stick?"

Danny cuffed me on the head and said, "Now you sound like an idiot."

That was the Danny I knew.

I walked him to his truck, only then asking him how Jack was doing.

"He's doing fine. He's spending the whole night inside tonight. First time. Saturday, I'm going to pick you up early and take you over there."

"What for?"

"You teach those girls at nine, right?"

"I'm sure Melinda is still down south, but Ellen, yes."

"Be ready by six. We'll get to Vista del Canada by seven with time to spare."

That was a reason to let him out of the gate, latch it, and run inside to study. The time you spend studying goes verrrryyy slowly while you are doing it, but after you've done it, it seems to have passed very quickly. I'm not sure why that is. At any rate, by Saturday morning, all thoughts of the Romans, the volume of a sphere, poems by dead people, French irregular verbs, and kingdoms, phyla, classes, orders, families, genera, and species had vanished from my brain.

Halfway there, it got light enough that I could see that it was a beautiful day—completely clear and bright, and the air had an extra sparkle that it sometimes gets in December. When we drove down the road that led to Vista del Canada, we kept seeing scarves of fog wafting against the mountainsides, and the mountains themselves looked like flat cutout layers receding against the pale sky. Everything was sleepy along that road until we went through the Vista del Canada gate, and there everything was busy as could be. Horses, riders, and grooms were everywhere. At the upper barn, all three wash racks were busy—cross-tied horses being sprayed, the spray foaming up in the morning sunlight, and the horses shaking their heads. In the hillside pastures, the mares were grazing.

Encantado was trotting back and forth in his paddock, staring at the four horses and riders making their way around the big white oval, one at the trot and three at the gallop.

The trotting one slowed to a walk, then went out the gate, and one of the cantering ones eased to the trot. Yet another was being ponied—a man on a palomino was trotting around the track, holding the lead rope of a bay, who was trotting next to him. The center of the track was empty. In the walking area, three grooms were leading their horses, who were enveloped between their ears and their swishing tails by swaying yellow coolers with green trim that had VISTA DEL CANADA embroidered into one corner and LEAMANN RACING embroidered into the other corner.

Danny parked and we jumped out. I followed him to a pen not too different from our training pen at home—a little smaller, with perfectly smoothed footing, as if one of the grooms had raked it by hand. Right when we got there, three guys came over, leading Jack, and he had a saddle on his back.

Yes, he whinnied when he saw me, and Roscoe Pelham and the other two brought him over to the fence so that I could pet him. I tickled him the way he always liked it, around the eyes and underneath his cowlick, and then down his cheek. It was really strange that he was wearing a bridle. It was a racing bridle, simple, with no noseband, but strange anyway. His mouth worked a little around the bit, but he seemed more interested than uncomfortable. Roscoe said, "Here's the owner, boys, Abby Lovitt. Abby, this is Wayne Griffin, the rider, and you know Ike."

I nodded. Wayne Griffin was not as tall as I was, but bald and strong-looking. When he smiled, I saw he had about eight teeth. He said, "Nice colt. Nice colt indeed." Then he stuck his hand out for me to shake. His hand was twice as big as mine and his forearm bulged with muscles.

Roscoe said, "Ready?" and Ike started leading Jack around and around the little pen, just walking. Roscoe and Wayne walked alongside Jack, step by step, with Roscoe occasionally patting Jack on the shoulder or putting his hand on his haunch. For a while, Jack was looking around—either over at the track or, when Encantado whinnied, in his direction. But he got bored with that.

Danny said, "He's been in here every day for the last three days. Yesterday, Wayne walked alongside him for twenty minutes." Danny leaned his elbows on the railing and stared.

The three of them stopped and stood there for a moment, then Roscoe and Ike stepped away from Jack, and Wayne started petting him and leaning against him. Jack didn't seem to care. All of a sudden, Wayne jumped on top of him, his chest in the saddle, his feet dangling, and his head on the other side. He stayed that way for a moment, petting Jack on his far side with his hands—Jack moved around, then stood still, and Wayne slid off. Then Wayne and Jack walked a little more, and Wayne did it again.

They came around to our side of the pen, and Wayne got on him a third time, but this time, he swung a leg over, and lay there, his feet hanging down and his chest along Jack's neck. Jack walked forward about three steps, but didn't make a fuss, and Wayne slid off again.

The reins were loose. Roscoe stayed near them.

Now they walked around again, and Roscoe and Wayne both stayed close to Jack, petting him sometimes and otherwise chatting and walking like there was nothing happening. Finally, they stopped, and Wayne petted Jack on the shoulder and the haunches, then launched himself again. He was a small guy, but he had a lot of spring. Now he lay forward for a few moments, and as Jack walked, he sat up and picked up the reins, and let Jack keep walking. Jack's ears were flicking back and forth, but he was walking easily—I was sure there were some horses who would stop or balk in surprise, but not Jack—his idea would always be to go go go. And now Wayne was going with him. That, I could see, was the perplexing part for Jack. Roscoe walked alongside for a few steps, then Jack and Wayne went around on their own. Just before Jack had the thought of "I don't like this," Wayne slid off, and they kept walking.

A few minutes later, they stopped, and Wayne jumped on again, but that didn't mean Wayne landed with a thump—he landed easy as you please, sat up, found his stirrups, walked along. There was nothing difficult about it. It was boring. It was supposed to be boring. It was only exciting if you thought about one of two things—the day you found that foal in the lower pasture, standing by his mom in the half darkness, or what it meant to be a racehorse, to have a name like Jaipur or Nasrullah, who was Jaipur's sire, or Bold Ruler, who was Jaipur's brother, or Yardstick, who was Mr. Matthew's horse. Danny and I had never seen a race, but Mr. Matthews had sent us some pictures after visiting us, and they were all of Jack's relatives getting to the finish line, their heads down and their noses out, galloping as hard as they could and beating some other horse. They didn't have to be moving in order to be exciting—a plain old black-and-white picture was enough. We'd looked at them then and forgotten about them, but now, between Jack and Gee Whiz, the whole thing seemed much more real and much more present.

"You brought him along nice," said Wayne as he passed us. "Don't nothin' excite him but his own self."

Roscoe laughed and they all kept walking. I didn't ask a single question, only watched them. After Wayne got off, he walked around on the other side from Roscoe, also giving some pats, and then they led Jack out of the pen to his stall, where they took off his saddle and bridle.

I followed them over there and gave him some carrot pieces. He took them and went back to his hay. He may as well have been talking—"No big deal. No big deal. What's the big deal?"

As we were leaving, Roscoe fell into step with us, and said, "Well, I hope Whiz is a good boy for you. When he started out, I thought he might be one of the big guys, but he bowed a tendon early in his three-year-old season. Not bad enough to end his career, but bad enough to end his Derby hunt. He came back as a four-year-old, and he's definitely been both useful and sound. Since he's a gelding, I let him go on as long as he seemed to like it, and that's been a long time. Can't count the occasions when Billy, that's our trainer down south, sent him out with one of our younger horses. His job was to set the pace and fade so the younger horse could come on and win. There were a couple of times he didn't fade!" Ross laughed. "But his last two races, Billy said, old Whiz seemed to be getting bored with the whole thing. We'll see

71

what's next." He shook my hand again, and headed for the upper barn, where, I think, the mares were.

On the way to the stables for Ellen's lesson, I thought I would have her mount a few more times, and tell her all about Wayne. Ellen liked to know what was possible.

We were there by eight-thirty, and for once, Ellen wasn't there ahead of us. Danny dropped me off, and I walked over to the main arena. The show season was over. The jumps now in the arena were not the freshly painted fancy ones but the day-to-day practice ones, which had scratches here, and missing branches there, and faded paint. For some reason, they weren't as imposing as the fancy ones. They seemed to say, "It's okay not to jump us perfectly. Lots of horses and riders have been over us hundreds of times, and they all got better eventually." Maybe that was reassuring.

Jane came up behind me, and said, "Oh, good. You're here. I have something to ask you. I've got some hot chocolate in my office, if you're chilled." She took my hand and felt it, then said, "Yes, you are. I could tell." I followed her into the office, and it was warm in there. She poured me a cup from a pot on her hot plate, and I closed my hands around it. She went behind her desk and sat down.

I sat down.

She said, "Melinda's mother called me."

I began to worry.

"She doesn't want her to stop taking lessons, but someone told her they could get quite a pretty penny for Gallant Man, and she wants to take advantage of that opportunity."

"Not Ellen's mom." This wasn't a question.

She shook her head.

"A pretty penny is not something the Leinsdorfs could afford. And I do believe that Melinda would be devastated if she couldn't take lessons. Her mother knows that. Anyway, the prospective buyer is in Los Angeles."

I must have sighed.

She said, "You should take that as a compliment. A reliable pony is a rare and valuable thing, and his fate is to move from child to child."

I nodded.

She said, "Anyway, I'm just warning you. The prospective buyer is coming to have a look this week, but there's many a slip between the cup and the lip."

I said, "People always say that, but I've never seen a single person pick up his cup and spill it before drinking it."

Jane laughed, then said, "Don't tell Ellen for now. Buyers from LA are very picky, and their vets never overlook the slightest thing. It's like they want it new out of the box but with years of experience and no mistakes. If they get to the vetting, I'll tell Mrs. Leinsdorf."

As I went out, I thought how different that was from the way my dad did it—he never called the vet. He went over the horse himself, with his own hands and his own eyes, checking for bumps and swellings and heat, looking for lameness, awkwardness, bad conformation, bad temperament. The people he sold horses to sometimes had them vetted, but usually everyone agreed that no horse was perfect, and if there was some problem, the question was, could you live with it?

Dad had a whole list of things he could live with, and a whole list of things he could not live with. But he never asked a vet, and we rarely called the vet, except for vaccinations and tooth-floating. Those were expensive enough. Some people would say it was luck, but Dad would say it was caution, plus letting horses live out the way they were meant to do, and added to that a diet of good hay and grass. And the grace of the Lord.

Outside the barn, Ellen was standing with Gallant Man and Rodney. She said, "I didn't let Rodney give me a leg up, because I practiced when I came out Wednesday." She turned around, gathered the reins, reached for the mane and the cantle of the saddle, and stepped onto Gallant Man. Then she said, "I'm getting good."

I said, "Yes, you are," and Rodney said, "You are, indeed, miss."

Ellen said, "Rodney, how old were you when you started to ride?"

"I was two, miss. Fell off and broke my leg out in a field when I was five. Took 'em three hours to find me."

I said, "What did you do all that time?"

"Oh, I stared at the clouds and sang some songs."

Ellen said, "When did you learn to mount from the ground?"

"Well, miss, for a long time, I was too small to do that, so I got my pony to side up to the fence, then I got on from there. I could stand with one foot on the post and one on the rail, and slip down onto the young fella."

Ellen said, "I don't believe you."

Rodney shrugged, then he said, "I practiced walking the fence rails after I saw the tightrope walkers in a traveling circus. For years, I planned to join the circus."

This shut Ellen up for at least half an hour—she did everything I asked as well as she could, and did not praise herself. When it came time to jump, I went over to the pony and put my hand on his neck. I said, "Did you believe what Rodney told you?"

She looked at me, then said, "I'm nine! That's old. I should have started as a child."

I said, "Well, you've made a good start, though."

She said, "Yes, I have, but still . . ."

I let her jump her little course five times, and she felt better.

The afternoon was cloudy and gray, but we had to get the horses ridden in case rain came and they were idle for days at a stretch. I went back and forth all afternoon fetching horses, putting them in the arena or the training pen, carrying tack, riding here and there, especially up along the hillside and on the trail to the Jordan Ranch, and I found that my eye was drawn to Gee Whiz time and again.

He certainly was a striking sight. We had put him with the other four geldings Friday morning, and he wasn't bad with them. It was more like he couldn't or didn't want to relate. He kept to his own pile of hay, kept to his own area of the pasture. Jack the Pest was no longer there, and the others saw the pinned ears and the raised hoof and understood their instructions—"Leave me alone." He did stand by the fence and watch the mares sometimes, his ears forward and his nostrils wide. Otherwise, when he wasn't eating, he was wandering around the pasture as if, actually, he was exploring it. He walked along the back fence line, sniffed the fence posts, nibbled the grass, looked up the hillside. He stood in the farthest corner, where no horse ever went, and stared off toward the Jordan Ranch. When birds landed on the fence or in the trees, he looked at them. He watched Rusty.

The other thing he did was roll. Every horse loves to roll, and every horse does so several times a day, but Gee Whiz rolled frequently, and always back and forth, from one side to the other, flailing his legs like a dog. As a result, he was dirty—his favorite rolling spots were the wettest ones. After two days, he was dirty from nose to tail. I pretended that this was not my business—this was not my horse, and no one was riding him, and so he didn't need to be cleaned up—but the fact was, I was like Dad. I preferred a clean horse, and there is no horse that shows the dirt more than a white one.

By suppertime, it was really gloomy, and then Dad said that he had heard on the radio that there would be snow.

Mom shivered and made herself a cup of tea. I wondered if I should suggest putting at least a few of the horses in for the night. I finally said, "That horse Gee Whiz doesn't have much of a coat."

"That's probably why they didn't clip him at the track. Good thing, or we would be blanketing him and unblanketing him all winter."

"But maybe he should go in a stall for the night."

Dad gave me that look that said, "How many times do we

have to talk about this?" then said, "It's not his hair that keeps him warm. It's his body and the soles of his hooves. If you went out there with just a little coat on, you would freeze to death, but that's because your surface area is very large compared to your weight. A horse is like a big football. His volume is huge compared to his surface area, and when he gets cold, he trots around. The trotting makes the soles of his feet vibrate, and they push the blood back up his legs and to his heart. If he's getting plenty to eat, and our horses are, he's warmer if he can move around than if he's stuck in a stall. That one can curl up pretty good, too. I saw him last night when I went outside—he was so bright you could hardly miss him. He had his legs all tucked up and his head and neck curled around. He's healthy. He'll be fine."

And, I thought, he has a nice coat of dirt on him to break the wind.

Hard Hat

Tall Boots

Chapter 5

Sunday morning, when we drove off to church, we did
see snow—not around us, but on the highest peaks, crusting
the grass and edging the tree limbs. Our oaks don't lose their
leaves in the winter, so to see the green and white sprinkled
together is oddly beautiful. It was our turn to bring some of
the food, so Mom had made two pecan pies and a pork roast.
They filled the back of the car with fragrance as we drove to
church, and the fragrance itself was warm and cozy.

Brother Abner was sitting in his seat when we got there,
smiling, holding his Bible. He stretched out his hand to me as
I walked past, and said, "Well, Ruth Abigail, it's nice to see
you again." I smiled and gave him a little hug, but Mom and I
exchanged a glance. He looked pale and thin. He didn't sing

along with the hymns, and when it came time for him to read his passage, he didn't stand up, the way he always had in the past. There was a long silence while everyone waited for him to open his Bible and start reading. Usually, Dad prepared his passage the night before, but Brother Abner always let the page present itself. I looked at Mr. Hollingsworth, who kept smiling, and at Dad, who continued to stare at his own Bible, and at Sister Larkin, who seemed worried. But finally, he let the Bible drop open and put his finger on the page, took a breath, and read, "When Isaac was old and his eyes were dim so that he could not see, he called Esau his older son, and said to him, 'My son'; and he answered, 'Here I am.' He said, 'Behold, I am old; I do not know the day of my death. Now then, take your weapons, your quiver and your bow, and go out to the field, and hunt game for me, and prepare for me savory food such as I love, and bring it to me that I may eat; that I may bless you before I die.'"

We knew this story—what happened next was that Esau's mother ran and got Jacob, her younger son, and had him kill a pair of goats, which Rebecca then cooked just the way Isaac liked them. She had Jacob take the dish of food to Isaac while wearing a piece of goatskin so that Isaac would touch him and think he was Esau, who was hairier than Jacob. When Isaac had eaten the food, he gave Jacob the blessing—that is, all of his things. Then Esau came back and found out that he was too late, and cried. I'd always thought this was a sad and confusing story, but after Brother Abner read his part, he paused a moment, and started laughing. Everyone smiled, the way you do when you are uncomfortable. Brother Abner finished laughing, coughed, and said, "Now, we all know what happened. There was a big fight, and it lasted for years and for generations. That's what happens when there is a big fight in the family—everything just feeds it, and pretty soon, no one knows why they're mad, they are just mad. Well." Now he shifted around in his chair, dropped his Bible, and reached down, very slowly, to pick it up again. I could see the sisters exchanging looks. He said, "What would have happened, I ask you, if Esau had done what old Isaac told him to do? If he'd taken his bow and his arrows and headed out into the wilderness, and made a new life for himself, instead of stewing and fussing? Or what if Jacob had stuck around, and had that fight with Esau, and taken his punishment and gotten it over with? What would have happened then? I tell you, everything seems important at the time, so important that you can't stand it if you don't do something, anything, to show how angry you are, how insulted you are. But then you get to be an old man, and you can't remember for the life of you what you were so mad about. An insult isn't an insult, you ask me now, it's just something that happens, most likely pretty funny, if you think about it." And then he got a little breathless, and sighed, and stopped talking. After another long pause, Brother Brooks stood up and read his passage, which was about Paul's epistle to the Romans.

It turned out that part of Brother Abner's problem was that the Studebaker wouldn't start, so Sister Larrabee had picked him up and brought him, and would take him home. She said to Mom, "Of course I don't mind doing that, and I told him that we'll go over to the Safeway and get a few things before we head out this afternoon, but really, I don't know what else to do. I did ask him on the way over here if he'd like a ride anywhere this week. Sister Larkin is happy to take him out, too, but he just waved me away."

Mom said, "Has anyone ever just dropped by there, just a friendly visit?"

"Oh, goodness, he knows none of us live in his neighborhood. He's pretty out of the way."

This year, Christmas would come on a Sunday. Our Christmas service the evening before would be by candlelight, and then we would have some Christmas food, like fruitcake and pumpkin pie. No presents, because some of the brothers and sisters were too poor to buy presents, so everyone else having presents would be embarrassing. I said, "At least, he won't be alone for Christmas."

"No, he won't," said Sister Larrabee, "and that's a blessing."

Mom said, "It's supposed to be so cold this week."

"I think I can spy a little bit on his wood supply. If it's low, I think I can mention that."

Mom nodded.

What Dad wanted to talk about on the way home was Esau and Jacob. He said, "Well, I've been thinking about that chapter of Genesis all day now. It's confusing. Of course, it doesn't apply to us, but it's funny that he happened on that one."

I said, "Who does it apply to?"

"Well, that's the biblical story of the Jews. The Jews all descended from Jacob, and the Gentiles all descended from

Esau. When Jesus came along, then a person could choose to follow the Lord of his free will, and it didn't matter about where you were born or who bore you. But I do remember, as a boy, just asking my dad over and over how it was that Jacob got away with it. To my mind, if he'd been in our family, he'd have gotten a whipping for sure. Finally, I was told that Jacob didn't really get away with it, since he had to run away to Laban's house. The important thing was that Isaac couldn't change his mind once he'd given his blessing. My dad said, 'There's the lesson in it for you—what's done is done, and you've got to make the best of it.' I think that's an important lesson, though whether Jacob and Esau made the best of it is a good question."

Mom said, "Well, it helps us to contemplate—"

"Our sins," said Dad. "Yes, that's true."

Mom said, "I was going to say our mistakes."

Dad said, "Looks like I have another one to contemplate."

Mom laughed, then said, "Not a very big one."

Monday, I woke up really happy, because Barbie was planning to come for a lesson in the afternoon. I didn't mind at all that even though it was still sunny and a little warm, you could see in the west that the clouds were building and the rain would be coming in. I didn't care that there would be three days, maybe, of cleaning tack and emptying old trunks and closets and saying, "Oh, I wondered where that bit had gotten to" and "I guess it's time to wash all the saddle blankets," because school was out and the Goldmans were home and Barbie had called me Saturday afternoon, and told me all about their concert, which had gone very well—another pair of students had sung a duet while Barbie and Alexis played violin and piano. I was sure that it had been beautiful and wished I'd seen it. She was due at three. I had no idea how her riding would be, so just to be safe, I tacked up Blue and rode him for half an hour before she got there. When she arrived, she was just herself—smiling and ready. We hugged for a long moment and then she hugged Blue. Her hair looked fine.

She was noticeably more skilled than she had been in the summer. Things I had once had to remind her of, like sitting up straight and keeping a loose back, and making sure that her heels were down but easily down rather than pushed down, were automatic for her now. She never even touched the horn of the saddle, and she sat the trot pretty well, though not perfectly.

I said, "Tell me again how often you rode Tooter?"

"Well, Tooter told me confidentially that four days a week was his preferred number, but I only managed three. He was nice about it, though."

"What about Alexis?"

"I have to say that Alexis got a lot of strange headaches when the time came to ride."

"Was she scared?"

Barbie asked Blue to halt in front of me, rested her arm on the horn of the saddle, and said, "I think she was, but she'd never tell me that. She's supposed to be the brave one. You and Blue should give her a lesson."

"If she asks, I will."

"May I canter again?"

"Of course."

"May I just canter around and around for the rest of the day?"

"His canter makes you want to."

"What I want to do is go for a trail ride, with a cantering part."

"We'd have to do that up on the Jordan Ranch."

"Could we?"

"If it's not too rainy. I haven't been up there for a couple of months."

She turned Blue away, went out to the rail, and cantered to the right. She sat easily, and Blue went at a smooth lope, his head up, his ears forward, and his back relaxed. It was hypnotizing. As they went past the far end of the arena, I could see Gee Whiz on the other side of the pasture fence, watching them. Each time they passed that way (they made four circuits), he snorted lightly and tossed his head. After the fourth time, he spun away and trotted off. He had a big, ground-eating trot, not loose but bold and proud. Blue, thankfully, either didn't notice or didn't care. Barbie brought him down to a walk and sighed.

She'd been cooling him out for about ten minutes when the rain started, first a foggy mist, then real drops. I wanted to get my saddle under cover, so I opened the gate, and we headed for the barn. By the time we got there—only a couple of minutes—it was actually pouring, and all three of us, Barbie, Blue, and myself, ended up kind of soaked. I was so busy trying to get under cover that I didn't notice Jerry Gardino's truck, but Beebop was cross-tied on the wash rack. Jerry was bending over, picking Beebop's right front hoof. He must have been cleaning him up for a while, because the horse's mane was smooth and his coat was shining. Beebop nickered when Blue came into the barn. Jerry stood up. He of course was smiling his big smile. He said, "Oh, hello!"

I said, "Barbie Goldman, this is Jerry Gardino, and this is Beebop, the wildest horse you've ever met."

Jerry said, "It's just a job for Beebop, not a way of life."

I said, "He's a bucking bronc in the rodeo. Jerry is his owner."

Barbie said, "Do you ride him?"

"God, no," said Jerry. "Dan said we might ride this afternoon. He was going to lend me Lady, I think it was, but it doesn't look as though that's in the cards." Outside, the rain was now falling in streams.

I said, "You'll have to cook something instead."

"What, though? I don't think the cannelloni went over very big."

"Oh, I love cannelloni," said Barbie. "Mushroom and ricotta. That's my favorite."

"I can do that," said Jerry.

I said, "Maybe it didn't look as though we liked it at dinner, but we polished off the leftovers. Mom and Dad kind of argued over who was going to get the last piece."

Jerry laughed, then he said, "Well, it came up that I might cook one last thing before vacation. That's why I'm here. I wanted to check on Beebop and clean him up a little, but I do think I mentioned something about veal piccata."

"Mmm," said Barbie.

I said, "You want to stay for supper?"

"Yes."

"Do you have to call home?"

"I do."

Jerry said, "Where do you live? I can give you a ride home after dinner. I'm heading straight up to the city."

I thought that Jerry Gardino and the Goldmans would get along perfectly, and probably they could compare recipes for hours. I said, "You can meet Alexis. She's Barbie's twin. Barbie plays the piano and Alexis plays the violin."

"Oh, really?" said Jerry. "I spent years playing the trombone in our school orchestra."

I said, "Was that fun?"

"It's fun until you lose count while you're sitting there waiting to come in. The guy who sat next to me fell asleep once."

Veal piccata turned out to have not only veal in it, but olive oil, lemon juice, butter, and parsley. Jerry spread his ingredients over every part of the counter, and made a terrible mess, but Barbie cleaned up after him, and so by the time we sat down, the kitchen looked fine. Mom thanked her, and she said, "It's just like when my mom cooks. I don't know what she's done without me all fall."

Dad bowed his head, closed his eyes, and said, "Let us give thanks. Our heavenly Father, we give thanks for the bounty we are about to partake of and the friends that have joined us this evening. Amen." I didn't close my eyes—I was too interested in what Barbie, Jerry, and Danny would do. Danny bowed his head but kept his hands in his lap, Jerry closed his eyes but didn't bow his head, and Barbie stared at Dad. She looked away before he opened his eyes.

As soon as Dad reached for the serving fork, Jerry laughed and said, "My dad always told us that when he was growing up, there was never enough money for eight whole chops, so when they said grace, they always finished with, 'In the name of the Father, the Son, and the Holy Ghost, the guy that eats the fastest gets the most.' But really, the guy who stuck his fork in there first always got someone else's fork in the back of his hand." He laughed, Barbie laughed, Mom said, "My goodness," and Dad smiled but looked uncomfortable.

Danny said, "How many brothers were there?"

"Six. One a year, until my grandmother said she was tying the door to her bedroom shut, because she didn't have a key to the lock."

I realized that Jerry Gardino was a lot like Beebop—ready for anything. The veal was good, and the noodles were good, and Dad took the second-biggest helping, after Danny, but what was really interesting was that I don't think Mom and Dad had ever been outnumbered by kids at the dinner table before. Jerry, Danny, and Barbie chatted on and on about Bob Dylan and something called the Monterey Pop Festival, which was coming up, and had we ever been to the Monterey Jazz Festival? Both Barbie and Jerry loved that and had been twice—Jerry had seen Duke Ellington and Barbie had seen Big Mama Thornton. (I looked around the table—Danny had at least heard of the festival, and maybe Leah had taken him? Mom and Dad looked politely blank.) Jerry was a big fan of Pete Seeger, but Barbie preferred a new group called Jefferson

Airplane, from up in San Francisco, and Jerry said, yes, they had just gotten Grace Slick to sing with them, someone he knew knew her, she had been singing with the Great Society—everyone in that group was related to one another. What was going on in LA?

"As if I know," said Barbie. "We only communicate with downtown by means of smoke signals. But everyone at school has a copy of *Pet Sounds*."

Jerry said, "I didn't like that at first."

Danny said, "I did."

Dad got up and carried his plate to the sink.

Then Barbie turned to Danny and said, "Say, Leah told me yesterday that you got your draft notice."

And Danny said, smooth as pie, "Well, I did. Physical in two weeks—like January fourth, I think." He did not look at Mom or Dad, but I did. Dad, who was rinsing his plate, stiffened, and Mom took a deep breath.

Barbie said, "You could go to Canada. We know a guy who did that. My dad . . ."

And then she looked around and stopped talking.

There was a long silence, and then Jerry said, "Did you ever read *On the Road*? I loved that book. I've been reading *Big Sur*. I know where that cabin is. I'd like to drive down there sometime."

But now Barbie was more alert, and she said, "I think my mom read that."

Danny said, "I was going to tell you, Mom. I don't think it's a big—"

Mom got up and walked out of the room.

Normally, it was Dad who got upset about things, but now he said, "It had to happen. I don't think your mom is willing to accept that, but this comes as no surprise to me. It was just a matter of time."

He sighed, and headed after Mom. On the way out of the kitchen, he touched Danny's hair. I hadn't seen him do that since Danny was a head or more shorter than he was—that would be when I was about eight.

Danny, Barbie, Jerry, and I cleaned up the kitchen, then I walked with Barbie out to Jerry's car. Before she got in, she said, "Sorry." And gave me a hug.

I said, "I'll see you Wednesday." Wednesday was the slumber party. Danny explained to Jerry how to get to Barbie's house, and they left. It was cold outside, but I didn't let Danny go back in the house. I said, "There's nothing wrong with you, is there?"

"I don't want anything to be wrong with me. It's not like I haven't thought about this. I don't see any way out. I've listened to all the arguments. Believe me, Leah knows all the arguments. She goes to Berkeley, for God's sake. She is furious with me."

"I didn't know you were seeing her still."

"Well, we stopped for a while, but that was worse." Then he added, "Maybe not worse than what's going on now."

"You should have told Mom."

"I was going to wait until after Christmas, or maybe until after the physical, when I would know for sure."

"Are you mad at Barbie?"

"I was for a moment, but it did save me having to bring it up. It's like you're standing at the edge of the cliff and looking down, and maybe it's easier if someone comes up behind you and pushes you over."

Then I said, "Guys come back from Vietnam all the time. I think you're going to be one of those."

Danny kissed me on the forehead and we went into the house. I have to say that I hadn't thought about this in a couple of months, not since Mom said that she found out that Sister Larkin's cousin, who was on the draft board, was somehow "putting Danny's file at the bottom of the stack," and so, even though he had been eighteen for a long time, he hadn't been called up yet. When Mom and Dad talked to Danny about it, Danny said that he didn't know what to think about the war and he thought he'd like to see for himself. That was Danny all over—as Dad knew and Leah was probably now discovering, there was no telling him what to do. He was determined to make up his own mind.

Lots of families talked about the Second World War, and what their dads (and moms) had done, but Mom and Dad were too young for that—Mom was only eleven when the war started, and Dad was only twelve. Uncle Luke was a few years older than Dad, and by the time Uncle Matthew was old enough to sign up, the war was over. He got as far as boot camp in Missouri. All of my grandparents were born just before the First World War, but someone somewhere had been in the Spanish-American War—that was at the end of the 1890s. And so I supposed that Danny would be the first to go. I had a hard time imagining it, but I suspected that part of the reason Danny wasn't all that upset was that he would see the world, or some of it. I could see how that would excite him.

Mom was sitting in the living room with her knitting in

her lap, and Dad was thumbing through his Bible. No one at church ever talked about the war—for one thing, no one but Danny was the right age to be drafted, and for another, all the older sisters and brothers disagreed. Brother Abner said what was going on over there was none of our business, and Sister Larkin said that the Lord worked in mysterious ways, and Mr. Hollingsworth said that stopping communism was the work of the Lord, and Sister Nicks and Sister Brooks had gone without speaking for four months after they disagreed about a passage Brother Brooks read that went "For though we live in the world, we are not carrying on a worldly war, for the weapons of our warfare are not worldly but have divine power to destroy strongholds." Brother and Sister Brooks said that as long as the Lord himself had brought up this passage by directing Brother Brooks to it, then they would express their view that it was not our job to fight the wars of the world, those of Lyndon Baines Johnson. Our battles were different. Sister Nicks had asked whether we were citizens of this country or not, and that had started it. It was now almost three years since that argument, and no one had ever said another word about the war. I knew that the teachers at school disagreed, too, but they did not talk about it in class.

Danny sat down beside Mom on the couch and put his arm around her, but he didn't say anything.

Dad said, "The future will unfold as it is meant to do."

Mom sighed.

Danny sat there for a while, and then kissed Mom on the cheek and left. I went up to my room and turned the stereo on pretty loud and read something.

It was my turn to get up in the morning to feed the horses. My alarm was set for six, a little later than usual, because there was no school and I didn't have to catch the bus. It was pretty dark at six. We'd talked about the winter solstice in seventh-grade science, and traced the apparent path of the sun. What it looked like that last week before the solstice was that it just made a little oval from the southeast to the southwest. The rays started out really long and cold and didn't get much shorter and warmer. I knew we were lucky compared to lots of places, but just because you are lucky doesn't mean that you feel lucky. Anyway, it seemed like it took me forever to pull on my socks and my jeans and my five shirts and sweaters and my hat and my gloves, and I was yawning the whole time, but I woke up when I opened the back door and stepped out on the porch. Right there in the yard, standing and looking at me, maybe ten feet from the back porch, was Gee Whiz. When I stopped with the back door in my hand, staring at him in surprise, he nickered, just like he was saying, "We're hungry."

I turned and looked at the kitchen clock. It was six-thirty. Other than Gee Whiz standing there, everything in the yard seemed normal—quiet, the sky pale the way it got just before sunrise. I put on my boots, and went down the steps. He stood still as I approached him. I petted him down the neck and took hold of his forelock, to get him to turn with me and go back to the barn, which was closer than the gelding pasture, but he didn't need pulling—he just pivoted and followed me, arching his neck, flaring his nostrils, and snorting slightly, as if he wanted a good whiff of me. He truly was the most curious horse I'd ever known.

We walked to the barn. From there, I could see that the gate of the gelding pasture was open, but not wide open—Gee Whiz had pushed it far enough to get through. Blue, Marcus, Lincoln, and Beebop were standing just inside, but they hadn't come out because, yes, Rusty was sitting in the opening, perfectly straight and alert. When Blue looked at me and stepped forward, she barked one short, sharp bark that said, "Stay!" in every language, including Horse. I led Gee Whiz toward them, but when I took a halter off the gate and turned to put it on him, just to make sure that I got him through without problems, he twisted his head away and trotted to the mare pasture. The mares, of course, were all eyes and ears— nothing more exciting than a loose horse—and they snorted and whinnied when he approached. I closed the gelding gate. Rusty gave a sigh, as if she were glad that her job was done, and she received several pats from me. There was no telling how long she'd been guarding the gate.

Gee Whiz would not allow me to catch him. He had to sniff noses with each mare in turn decide—like everyone, I suppose—that Oh My was the best-looking, since he snorted and arched his neck when he came to her.

For once in my life, I didn't have a single carrot in my pockets, so I ran to the barn and got a small bucket with a few handfuls of oats. This I shook as I came back to him, and he did prick his ears, and he did take a bite while I was opening the gate again, and he did allow me to lure him inside the pasture (waving off the other geldings, of course). I then stood with him while he ate the rest of the oats, because even though he had been naughty, he had been good to follow me and needed to be rewarded. All the horses were staring at me now, and the reason was that I was late with breakfast.

After I passed out the hay, I inspected the gate latch. It was a simple one—just a piece of wood that slid through a space in the frame of the gate, and then lodged itself into a carved-out slot in the gatepost. The latch was old and unpainted, not that easy to move. I fiddled with it while the horses ate, and I decided that in the excitement of the night before, someone hadn't closed it properly (maybe me). I made sure the latch was very firmly in its slot, and even jiggled it. I decided that the episode had been a little scary, but easy to understand, so I also decided to just put it out of my mind—lots of times there are near misses with horses. If you didn't put them out of your mind, your mind would fill up and overflow.

Lead Rope

Halter

Chapter 6

When I got inside, Mom was up, making oatmeal. She still didn't look very happy, but I took the cowardly way out and decided that this wasn't my business. She set my oatmeal on the table, and I reached for the milk. I said, "You remember the slumber party tomorrow night, don't you?"

She nodded, and said, "Oh yes."

"Did you talk to Dad about it?"

"I did. It's okay for you to go, but he wants to pick you up before breakfast Thursday morning so that you can get your riding done."

"Did you explain to him what a slumber party is? People stay up late."

"I mentioned that, but he didn't seem to notice."

She stared at me. I could see that her mind was working. Finally, she said, "I think we need to do some Christmas shopping. I think it absolutely has to be done Thursday morning. I think it's an emergency."

We smiled at one another. I said, "What time do you think you'll be finished with that?"

"Oh, about noon."

When you went to the Goldmans', you never knew what was going to happen. Once, we'd put on an amateur (very amateur) performance of *Julius Caesar*; once, we had played a game where you had to act out an adverb, like "crazily," and your team had to guess what it was; and of course, at the end of the summer, we'd had a scavenger hunt through the neighborhood. You also never knew why a particular person might have been invited to a Goldman party (and actually, I wondered why they had originally invited me—Barbie said it was because I was mysterious, which I suppose meant that I spent years trying to keep out of everyone's way as best I could). Now, of course, we were friends, and I loved having Barbie come and ride Blue. She was easy to give lessons to— she always did what she was told, and she was *able* to do what she was told, which is a separate thing.

Sophia was arriving as Mom and I turned into the Goldmans' street. The Cougar that her mom drove was inching along, no doubt because they were looking at street numbers. Mom eased around them and went into the Goldmans' driveway, and I jumped out and waved. Mrs. Rosebury pulled in behind us. Maybe I expected Sophia to be nervous—she didn't know the Goldmans, though she had seen them a long time ago in a play—but if she was, I couldn't tell. She was her usual self—she might as well have been walking into geology as into the Goldmans' house. Barbie met us at the door before we rang the bell, as if she'd been watching through the window. She hugged me, and shook Sophia's hand, then said, "I'm so happy to meet you! Abby says that your equestrian style is perfect! She gives me lessons, you know, but I have a long way to go."

Sophia smiled. Good beginning. Another interesting thing was that Sophia's hair was loose rather than in her usual thick braids. It was blond and smooth and rippled down her back as she walked. It fell to her waist. Stella would have been full of compliments.

Being in the Goldmans' house was almost like not being inside a house at all. The living room had a huge window that looked out over a big valley—now the valley was utterly dark, and the sky above and beyond the edge of the hills was brilliant red-orange. We set down our overnight bags next to three others. Sophia had brought a sleeping bag, and I had brought what Mom called a bedroll, which was really just a blanket and a sheet folded together and rolled up. Doors at either end of the window opened out onto a deck. I could see Leslie, Alexis, and a girl I didn't know out there. Leslie waved to us and Sophia waved back.

To the left of the living room was a big kitchen, and to the right was Mr. Goldman's study. I saw that the furniture had been pushed aside, so this would be where the slumber party would take place, not upstairs in Barbie and Alexis's rooms. (There were two—they slept in one of them in bunk beds, and had their musical instruments and a table of art supplies in the other one. They were the only kids I'd ever known who had been allowed to decorate their own rooms, by painting pictures on the walls—I hoped Sophia would get to have a look.) Staccato was curled up on a pillow on the couch. He'd put on weight in the last few months, and looked like a grown-up cat. When we'd found him in the spring, Mom thought he was less than a month old, so he was still only about nine months. But he was relaxed. When I tickled the top of his head, he rolled over and displayed his belly. He started purring immediately. I said to Barbie, "Does Staccato ever do anything? Every time I see him, he's relaxing."

"He caught a fly yesterday. But it was a very slow-moving fly."

The doorbell rang and she went to answer it. Another girl I didn't know came in, followed by Lucia. Barbie must have said something funny, because they started laughing, and then smiled at us and said, "Hi!"

Mrs. Goldman came down the stairs, smiling, and said, "Oh, how nice to see all of you girls! How are you? You look so grown-up!" She gave everyone a kiss on the cheek and went into the kitchen.

As we drifted out onto the deck, Lucia said, "I was wondering who would be here!" I suspected not Stella and Gloria, and by the time everyone had arrived, I saw that I was right. One surprise was that Leah did come, and why not? She was their cousin even if she was four years older and in college. She gave me a hug that said all sorts of things from "I think I love your brother" to "What is going to happen now?" But Leah was quiet—at Goldman parties, she never said much, though she drew funny pictures on napkins and showed them to you sometimes. It was a sign of how much fun the Goldman twins were that Leah had decided to show up.

On the deck, there were five artichokes set on two tables, ready for the leaves to be plucked and dipped in five sauces. I could tell that one was melted butter. The others were white, green, red, and brown. There were two cheeses, neither of which looked like anything I'd seen before (they were white), and there was a long loaf of bread. I must have been staring at the food, because Leslie came up behind me and said, "I recognize the olives and the almonds." She took one of each.

Leslie had on her favorite sweater, which was blue-green and had a boatneck. She was wearing it with very dark blue wool pants that I had never seen before—buttons came up one side, crossed under the waist, and went down the other side. I said, "Where did you get those pants?"

"They're navy surplus. They're what sailors wear."

She stepped back. The bell-bottom legs were so big it looked like she could trip on the hems. She turned around. A string like a shoestring was threaded through holes that ran up the back. And they did fit her nicely. She said, "If I fell off my ship, I could get these off over my shoes, and then tie the legs, throw them upward to capture some air, and use them as sort of a life raft. Then I would take off my shoes." I was sure that she would survive. She did look good—willowy and "understated," as Stella would say.

Alexis made introductions. Other than Sophia, Leslie,

Lucia, Leah, and me, there was Diana (Alexis's roommate from school); Ingrid, a cousin of Diana's from Norway; and another girl from school who hadn't gone home for vacation, Marie. Marie was French. I did not dare say *bonjour*, even though I'd been taking French for three years. Marie was staying for a couple of days, until she left to meet her parents in Aspen, Colorado, to go skiing. Sophia said, "I went to Paris once, with my mom and dad. I can't remember it very well, though."

Marie smiled, and said, "I am from the South. From Toulouse. My father teaches in the university there."

None of us had maybe ever heard of anywhere in France except Paris, and wherever it was Joan of Arc was from. Alexis said, "Marie is a great skier." Marie shrugged slightly, then helped herself to a piece of the white cheese. Ingrid, as it turned out, spoke German, French, and Norwegian but not English, so she chatted with Marie in French. Neither of them sounded at all like our French teacher, Madame Desmond— or Madame Defarge, as she was called behind her back. Sometimes, when she was being very strict, a couple of the boys would pretend to be knitting.

Diana and Ingrid had come down from San Francisco just for the party because, as Diana said, "Every time I tell my folks about Alexis and Barbie, they roll their eyes as if I'm making it up. I had to bring an independent witness." I started liking her right then. Diana's talent was math. The Jackson School had already given up on teaching her, and she went three times a week to UCLA for classes. She said, "There was a school I could have gone to in SF that had high-level math classes, but my folks also wanted me to learn how to tie my shoes and put the cap back on the toothpaste."

Alexis said, "We've been working on that. If I were your mom, I would settle for you not sitting on your glasses every other day."

Diana laughed.

Mrs. Goldman came out carrying another dish—this one was a metal frame with a pot sitting on it. Under the pot was a flame. In the pot was something thick and liquidy. Marie said, "Ah, *très bon! Fondue au fromage!*" A moment later, Mrs. Goldman came out with another plate, this one of pieces of carrots and broccoli and green beans. Marie and Ingrid sat down at once and started tearing apart the loaf of bread, sticking pieces onto the prongs of long forks, and dipping them into the cheese (I did know what *fromage* was). The rest of us sat down with them. Surprisingly, Sophia, who hardly ever ate anything, dipped three pieces of bread and ate them, then tried a carrot and a green bean. Leslie and I looked at each other—we spent a lot of lunch hours watching Sophia eat and offering her things we thought she might (should) like.

Mrs. Goldman brought in another pot. This one had bubbling oil in it (we had to move out of the way when she set it on the table). Then she brought in a plate of beef cubes and two sauces, one that was orange and sweet and another that looked like barbecue sauce. She told us not to have more than six forks in either pot, or the fondue would cool off, so we took turns. I did like the cheese, and I did like the beef without sauce or with a little of the barbecue sauce. Leslie ate a little bit of everything, and Sophia ate two pieces of beef and two more chunks of bread and cheese.

Dinner by fondue takes a while, and the whole time, we were talking. Marie told about skiing in the Alps and the Pyrenees. Ingrid talked about how wonderful it was to see ten hours of daylight so close to Christmas (Diana translated for her, and said that in Oslo, the sun was coming up at about nine-thirty and going down at about three). Leslie said that she was running three miles without stopping for a rest, and had heard about a thing called a marathon, and then it turned out that a marathon was twenty-six miles. Sophia told about Onyx and Pie in the Sky. Barbie told about Blue and Tooter, and Alexis said that there was a teacher at the high school who taught scuba diving, and explained what that was, and that was a reason she wanted to come back and go to our high school. Lucia said that she had taken that course in the summer, and that the bay, which we could walk to from school, was actually a deep canyon—two miles from the surface to the bottom in some spots, and even below the water, as deep as the Grand Canyon. I had been sitting at lunch with Lucia for ages, but she was so quiet that I didn't know any of this. Leah asked if we remembered a show on TV called *Sea Hunt*, but no one did. Leah said that everyone in Berkeley was a vegetarian, and ate something called tofu, which was made of soybeans and came in various shapes, like chicken legs and liver and Mars bars. I told about Gee Whiz's career at the racetrack, and about his getting out of the pasture and coming to stand by the porch while Rusty prevented the other horses from escaping.

The conversation went in fits and starts because we were also trying to dip our forks and not spill. There could have been some sort of bragging, since I had the sense that everyone there was quite good at something or other, but there wasn't—bit by bit, everyone loosened up, so that by the time Mrs. Goldman brought the last pot, we were laughing most of the time. The last pot was chocolate, dark and thick, and incredibly wonderful-smelling. We got little cubes of angel food cake to dip into it. Marie said that her favorite *fondue au chocolat* was with strawberries and raspberries. I could only imagine it. We did make kind of a mess with the chocolate fondue.

When we went back into the living room and Alexis turned on the lights, I saw that they had set out a large white mat with rows of brightly colored spots on it. "Oh," said Leslie, "Twister!" And indeed, TWISTER was written across one edge. There were ten of us, too many for one game, so we took numbers out of a bowl. Numbers 1 through 4 began the game while number 5 twirled the spinner and told each participant where to put each hand or foot. When an elbow or a knee touched the mat, or someone fell, she was out; the next number came in, and the first open number took over twirling the spinner. While we played the game, the stereo was on, a stack of records of all kinds, including the Rolling Stones and the Lovin' Spoonful, but also Martha and the Vandellas, Ray Charles, and an old record of Marie's by Edith Piaf. There was even one my dad might have liked, Patsy Cline. The music made it more fun, and pretty soon we were all dancing around and shouting if we weren't playing.

Sophia got number 3, and of course she was good at the game—she could twist most of the way around but hold herself perfectly still. She outlasted numbers 1, 2, 4, 5, and 6, and maybe she only buckled then because she was tired. I was number 7. My first turns were very easy, mostly like crawling across the mat, but then I had to reach my right hand under my body and put it way past my left foot, and I fell over, knocking over Ingrid. Leslie ended up completely upside down, her hands and feet spread wide, looking upward, and after she had been there for a while, Barbie started counting out seconds to see how long she was going to last—she made it to thirty-six seconds, which seemed like a lot, and then she started laughing when Alexis ran a feather up her right bell-bottom and tickled her on the leg. Even laughing, she lasted another eight seconds, which was, I said, as long as you were supposed to stay on a bucking bronco, and then Barbie had me tell them about Beebop, her "future mount."

I think we made it through the Twister lineup two and a half times before Alexis brought out the playing cards and started telling our fortunes with a dish towel wrapped around her head, and Barbie standing behind her mouthing the words "Don't believe a thing she says!" Her predictions were that Marie was going to go skiing, I was going to go riding, Leslie was going to run three miles, and Sophia was going to go on a trail ride with Barbie and have to save her life by galloping alongside her and dragging her off her horse as they galloped toward a cliff while an earthquake was taking place.

"And a thunderstorm!" exclaimed Diana.

"And a tornado!" shouted Lucia.

"And a Martian attack!" exclaimed Leslie.

Barbie said, "I don't see any problem, really."

And then I fell asleep.

It may be that I was the only one at the party used to going to bed before ten and getting up before six, and it also may be that I was the only one who as a rule slept like a log. I hadn't even unrolled my bedroll. I was lying on the couch watching the fortune-telling, and the next thing I knew, I was waking up and yawning, and the room was quiet and dark. Various mounds around me indicated that others were asleep, too, but one of these was not Barbie. I could see her with Sophia and Marie over in the corner, doing something. I yawned again, and Barbie turned around, put her finger to her lips, and waved me over. I crawled.

The corner was dim, but there was some light from the moon, which was big and bright outside the window. The three of them were sitting with their legs crossed about six or eight feet from Alexis, who was asleep in her sleeping bag. She was lying on her side, with one elbow bent, and her hand under her pillow. Her other arm was resting on her hip. The sleeve of her pajamas was kind of pulled up and twisted. As I looked at her, she made a little snore.

Barbie, Marie, and Sophia were kneeling around a pot of water, talking in very low voices. Barbie said, "It works. It worked at school. You stick the hand of the sleeping person in a pot of warm water, and it makes them say something. The thing they say is the truth. It's like hypnosis. You ask them a question in a really low voice, so as not to wake them up, and they tell the truth, no matter what they've been saying when they're awake."

Sophia was shaking her head. She said, "They don't tell

the truth. They wet their pants. The feeling of the water makes them wet their pants."

"It didn't do that at school."

"Did you do it to someone?"

"I didn't, but some other girls did, and four of the boys did it, too."

Marie said, "I'm not sure whether boys care enough about wetting their pants to remember if they did it."

We all laughed quietly. Apparently, Alexis was to be the victim.

I said, "What are you going to ask her? Didn't you always tell me you could read her mind, anyway?"

"I can read the good thoughts."

Marie said, "Alexis doesn't think bad thoughts."

Barbie said, "That's what I want to find out."

Sophia was still serious. She said, "If she wets her sleeping bag, it's very hard to get it out." She had put her hair into a loose braid that went down her back and looked comfortable. She was wearing a nightgown, yellow flannel with little teddy bears. I still had on my clothes, Marie had on shortie pajamas, and Barbie was wearing a T-shirt and a pair of long johns like my dad wore on very very cold days. She picked up the pot of water, which sloshed a little bit, and moved it closer to Alexis's hand. She put her finger in it, to test it. I put my finger in it, to test it. It was about the temperature of bathwater. We all crept closer to Alexis, who snored once again, and heaved a sigh. Once we were next to her, Barbie made a motion with her hand that we were to sit very still and not say anything. We sat like that for what seemed a long time, then Barbie slid her fingers underneath Alexis's fingers and kept them there. I found myself holding my breath, as if something bad was going to happen. We all waited, and then bit by bit, Barbie eased Alexis's hand toward the pot and slid it into the water. Alexis did not wake up. I glanced at Sophia. Her eyes were wide and blue in the moonlight.

Finally, Barbie leaned very close to Alexis. We all leaned in. Barbie whispered, "Where did you hide my cashmere sweater?"

I had to put my hand over my mouth not to laugh, and I saw Marie grin, too. But there was no answer from Alexis, just another snore. Barbie leaned in again and repeated the question. There was a moment of silence, and then Alexis muttered, "I sold it on the black market." We all laughed, even Alexis, who opened her eyes. She had been awake the whole time.

After that, we settled into our beds and gradually fell asleep. The last thing I heard was Marie and Alexis whispering about something.

You would have thought that the sun would wake us up—that room was so bright—but we slept all the way until Mrs. Goldman brought in a coffee cake with cinnamon swirls through it and brown-sugar crumbles over the top. She also had orange juice, hard-boiled eggs, and strips of bacon, and it was all very good—we sat around in our pajamas eating from paper plates. Some of the others said what they were going to do for Christmas—Sophia and her parents always went to the club that was attached to the stables and served a huge buffet. Leslie was going caroling with her cousins in a certain neighborhood not far from the high school that was famous for elaborate decorations—the three of them had already rehearsed their carols five or six times. Leslie sang alto. Lucia always went to midnight Mass (Marie's parents liked that, too—the town where they lived had a beautiful cathedral from about the year 1100, which was hard to imagine). Of course, the Marxes and the Goldmans did nothing for Christmas, but they had celebrated Hanukkah by eating potato pancakes. Ingrid said, through Marie, that in her family, they had a storytelling contest where they told traditional Christmas fairy tales about an elf called Fjøsnisse who plays tricks on Christmas Eve. I didn't say what we did, and no one asked, but I did look around and think that Dad would consider every single one of my friends "unsaved." He thought that going among the unsaved was necessary but dangerous. The fact was, I went among the unsaved all the time, but thinking about Christmas made it more obvious.

Around noon, we cleaned up after ourselves, and pretty soon, the cars started showing up. Mom was the only one driving a truck. As I opened the door to get in, Barbie said, "So, I'll come for my lesson tomorrow at two, but can we do one thing?"

"What?"

I thought she was going to say go for a trail ride or something, but she said, "Can we get Gee Whiz out and play around with him?"

This struck me as a really good idea, just the sort of idea that I should have come up with on my own. I said, "I'll ask Danny." But I was sure he would say yes, and I thought maybe he would show up, if he could. When we drove away (I was waving good-bye to everyone), the first thing Mom asked me about was what we'd had to eat—I told her about the fondues, especially the chocolate one, and the white cheeses. She had heard of fondue, but never seen it. Apparently, there was a restaurant somewhere not far away that served only fondue. She thought that it didn't sound very filling—she and Dad liked food that "sticks to your ribs." She and Dad had done a lot of shopping—we were on our way to pick him up at the hardware store. As she talked, I looked at her, and I looked around at the truck—it was old. The greatest thing about California, as far as Dad was concerned, was no ice and therefore no salt on the roads, so a car or a truck could last forever, say two hundred thousand miles, no problem, because no body rust. Uncle Matthew in Oklahoma had driven a car for years that had no floor on the driver's side—you could watch the road whizzing by underneath it—so when he started seeing Aunt Rhoda, he had put a piece of plywood in there somehow. Dad acted as though this was funny. I thought about spending the rest of my life driving around in a truck as old as I was. With, I found myself thinking, parents who never had fondue, would never go to Paris, or probably not Los Angeles, and maybe not even San Francisco. Mom was pretty and young, but she would never wear makeup, or a short skirt, or fishnet hose. I mean, there were lots of mothers who would never wear fishnet hose, but Mom, pretty as she was, would also never *have* worn them. And maybe, somehow, my parents had made of me the sort of person who would never wear them, either.

Truly, the most interesting person at the party was not, for once, a Goldman. It was Marie. I'd hardly said a word to her; she and I had smiled at each other a few times. But I watched her. Everything she did was good-natured, graceful, and smart. She had been to England and Italy and even Turkey and Morocco. Coming to school in Malibu, and adding to that a skiing vacation in Colorado, were easy as pie for her. I had never been on a plane. Mom had never been on a plane. Dad had never been on a plane. No wonder Danny didn't mind the thought of being drafted.

It took forever to get home, and after Dad got in beside me, they talked around me all the way home about candles for church and food—pot roast or turkey? What kind of potatoes? Mashed were good, but there were also baked and boiled. How about sweet potatoes? Which was more festive, and what did the brothers and the sisters like? When we drove through our gate, I jumped out when Dad got out to open it and went straight to the barn—not because I was dying to ride, but because I was dying to get away from my parents.

Jumping Chute

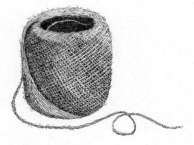

Baling Twine

Chapter 7

IT WAS ALREADY LATE, SO I DECIDED TO RIDE JUST ONE HORSE, purely for pleasure. Of course I chose Blue. He was standing by the gate, so all I did was open it, put a halter on him, and walk him to the barn. As we left the pasture, Gee Whiz let out a ringing whinny. I turned around, and he nickered, too. His ears were pricked, and he looked very handsome, his dark eyes in his white face. I glanced at Blue. Even in the short time we'd had him—since the late winter—he had shed out twice, and he was noticeably lighter than he had been a year before. He was now almost eight, we thought—that would be a year younger than Gee Whiz, but he was a good deal darker. You never knew with grays how quickly they would gray out, how quickly their stars and blazes and white stockings would disappear completely as the rest of the horse turned white.

Jane had told me about a horse she knew who was born a chestnut and stayed a chestnut for years, and then the spring when he was ten, his winter coat fell out, and he was white. That was rare—I'd never heard of anything like it. Every horse is born dark, but if a horse has a gray parent (and every gray horse has at least one gray parent), you can look at his eyelids and the area around his eyes and see gray hairs. That means he's a gray and will eventually turn white. If a gray parent produces a nongray colt or filly, then the gray has gone out of that line, because gray is a dominant gene—if it's there, you see it (we had learned about dominant and recessive genes in biology). Dad said that meant that the population of grays was always getting smaller, but I didn't know if that was really true. Lots of horsemen swore up and down that coat color and temperament were related—they had never seen a gray mare with a good temperament, or they said chestnuts were like redheads, sensitive and hard to handle. But in my experience, horsemen had lots of theories, and all of them changed when they bought another horse.

I cross-tied Blue and got my boots off the back porch. It was very nice just to say nothing and to have the only sounds I heard be Blue blowing out a little air, or even just breathing. Horses breathe in a comforting, serious way, and Blue, like all Thoroughbreds, had wide nostrils that seemed to be taking in a lot of air. His winter coat was thick, smooth, and silky, not at all fluffy. Even though he lived outdoors, he hardly had to be curried, and after I brushed him with the soft brush, I polished him with my favorite chamois. He always liked that best. Then I very carefully combed his mane, which was a little long for the winter, but not terribly tangled. I took the twigs and the burs out of his tail, but I didn't brush it—I would save that for the show season. Even Rodney, out at the stables, didn't brush horses' tails except for the show season. He said, "A long hair that gets yanked out takes a fair long time to grow back."

I put my English tack on him, and thought, as usual, that I needed to clean it, and then I led him out of the barn toward the arena. Almost immediately, another loud whinny rang out. I turned. It was Gee Whiz again. His whinny was distinctive—sharp and steady, like the note of a brass instrument. Dad didn't think that horses were saying anything with their whinnies, and maybe they weren't saying "See you later" or "Watch your step," but I knew that their whinnies were so individual that they were saying "This is me." Blue didn't answer.

I had spent a lot of time doing groundwork with Blue, and I considered him trained enough now that I could get on, ride a little bit, and then decide if I needed to get off, so I sided him up to the fence, climbed to the third rail, and mounted. Then I loosened him up at the walk by stepping him over in both directions, asking him to back, doing a few spirals in each direction, and then something Jane called a turn on the haunches and Danny called a spin, where you ask the horse to steady his back legs and pivot his front legs around them. Then a few figure eights, then some long strides and short strides, then the trot. Blue moved along agreeably. Every so often, he looked at something—a bird flying, or Rusty up the hill, watching us (and everything else). The fourth time we

117

went around the end of the arena near the barn, I saw that Gee Whiz had stationed himself at that end of the pasture again.

I realized that I had never known a horse who was so determined to communicate something. All the time I was looking at him, and thinking thoughts about him, I now realized, he was looking at me (or us, maybe just humans in general) and thinking thoughts about us. He was a horse who wanted something. Since he had water and food and equine companions, since he was no more or less interested in pieces of carrot than any of the others, I realized that it had to be something else, something that he thought only humans could give.

But I went back to concentrating on Blue. At the trot, we did some more figure eights, then a long curlicue that Jane called a serpentine. We did some big loops, then a pattern that I thought of as a shamrock, not so different from a figure eight. We practiced transitions from the walk to the halt, the walk to the trot, the trot to the halt, the walk to the canter, and then the halt to the canter. I tried asking him to back, then asking him to canter on the left lead, then backing and asking him to canter on the right lead. He did everything very nicely, and, in fact, he did backing and then cantering beautifully, as though he particularly enjoyed it, even though we'd started working on it just a few days before. We cantered and galloped and cantered and galloped both directions, then counter-cantered, which Jane said he had to know. Counter-cantering is, basically, cantering on the wrong lead. If you ask a horse to do it, it's a good exercise, since it helps him stretch his muscles and learn good balance. While we were doing all of these things, I got into that state of mind I always did when he was good, very calm and smooth, almost like dreaming, in a way, where I felt his body moving under me, and I also felt the way his feet stepped and the movement of the air as I passed through it. I was aware of the sun and the trees and the railing of the arena, of the jumps and the cones and the other things in the arena, but mostly I sensed the swaying of the two of us together, moving.

When we were done with all of these exercises, I gave him a long rein and we walked around the arena, relaxing. I petted him by gently taking his mane in my hand and running my fingers along the top of his neck. And I said, "Well, True Blue, I think you're trained."

I hadn't meant to say this, and my first feeling when I heard myself was to feel a little proud—he had, after all, learned all of his lessons and gone, in nine months, from a well-meaning but ignorant mystery horse to a cooperative and knowledgeable friend. I didn't plan to jump, but I had jumped that week, and he had learned that pretty well, too—he didn't love it, but he did a good job over modest jumps, gauging his takeoff, making a nice arch, and landing in a well-balanced way. I might have wanted him to be like Onyx or Pie in the Sky, to have the sort of spring and talent that made onlookers gasp, but he didn't have that. Jane and I thought that maybe 3'3" was his optimum height. Above that, even if he could do it (and Ralph Carmichael thought any horse was capable of four feet, but Jane said this was a very old-fashioned cavalry and English fox hunting way of thinking, and if I never saw horses in a hunt field crashing through a fence or falling over one, that would be good), he would not feel happy doing it— he would only be doing it because he had to.

He was good about siding up to the gate and standing quietly so that I could bend down to open it. We walked back to the barn. Dad was there, tacking up Lady. He said, "I watched you two for a few minutes. That horse is a completely different animal. You've done a good job with him." In the barn, Dad looked like himself, tall and thin, with big shoulders, wearing his work hat with the brim rolled up at the sides, working around a horse as if it were the most natural thing in the world. I thanked him and gave him a little hug. He didn't know what the hug was for, but it was for just being himself.

It was Ellen who called Jane, not her mom. Jane was laughing that night when she called me, to see if we could reschedule the normal Saturday lesson. According to Ellen, "Christmas Eve is a very busy day, and I'm not sure I'm going to be able to concentrate, so I would prefer to take my lesson tomorrow." Barbie was coming at two o'clock, so I asked Mom if she could take me to the stables at ten, and she said she could, because then she could pick up the turkey and the parsnips, and hadn't we once served . . .

I tuned the rest out, but I did keep nodding and smiling.

And Ellen did concentrate, as only Ellen could. Her trot circles were round, her figure eights had identical halves, her transition to the canter was at just the right spot, and her canter down the long side was even and rocking. She didn't have to be asked to pet her pony, and I didn't have to be asked to set the jumps at two feet, which was exciting enough for Ellen, totally routine for the pony, and not too exciting for me (I could just imagine something going wrong, but I tried not to). The arena we were using was a rectangle, so I set a jump in the middle of one end, another one about halfway down one side, and a third one about halfway down the other side. The first exercise was to do small circles in both directions, at the trot and at the canter, taking in each jump as she went around the circle. She did this very neatly. The second exercise was to do all three jumps, first to the left, then to the right, letting the pony pick his own comfortable gait. He picked the canter. The third exercise was to canter to the right over the three jumps, make a big loop after the last one, and then go back the other way. The pony landed on all his proper leads, and Ellen stayed with him the whole time, her heels down, her eyes up, and a smile on her face—the judge likes to know you are having a good time. She was good. He was very good. Or at least, that's what she told Jane when we got back to the barn. Jane laughed and patted her on the head, then she said to me, "If you've got a minute." But of course she knew I had plenty of minutes. As I walked into her office, I could hear Ellen telling Rodney in detail about every single jump, and Rodney saying, "You're joking me, miss. Surely you didn't do that!"

Jane sat on the edge of her desk and sighed a little sigh, then said, "The pony vetted out fine. They'd like to ship him down to LA the day after Christmas. That's Monday. And they don't want to take any chances, so he's to stay in his stall except for Rodney walking him out every day. He's suddenly gone from being a very nice pony to being a very valuable pony, so he won't be allowed to do anything on his own, without plenty of padding, I'm sure." She looked at me and shook her head. "I know a woman in Maryland. She has a beautiful place with wonderful pastures and the best possible fencing, but she will not put the horses out because they are so valuable, and she's so afraid one of them might get hurt!" Then she said, "Well, it's not my business." She looked right at me, and said, "That stall will be empty for five days after the pony leaves. I want you to consider something."

"What?"

"I want you to consider bringing Blue over here and letting Ellen and Melinda ride him. Melinda will be back Monday."

I said, "I don't think my dad could afford keeping him here."

Jane said, "Well, we'll see. But you know, I haven't seen him since the clinic. I miss him. I want to see what you've done with him. The stall is paid for, and I'll give you a free lesson in the big arena. How would that be?"

That, I thought, would be great.

When we were finished talking, I walked over to Gallant Man's stall to say good-bye. He was staring into the distance, chewing a mouthful of hay, and he nickered at me when I approached. Ellen and I had already given him all of our bits of carrots and lumps of sugar, so I went around behind the barn and pulled a few hanks of green grass, which he took from me very nicely. I scratched him under his mane and tickled him around his forelock, which he liked. There had been a time, not so long before, when I'd had to reach up to tickle his fore-lock, but that wasn't true anymore. I said, "You are such a Gallant Man. I wish you weren't a pony." We had called Gallant Man just "the pony," but Jane had named him after a very small horse who'd won the Belmont Stakes. He had also almost won the Kentucky Derby, but his jockey thought they'd crossed the finish line and stood up in his stirrups. But the horse hadn't yet crossed the finish line—another horse came up and beat him by a nose. Jane had seen two of Gallant Man's races when she lived in the East, and she thought our pony had some of his "sass," as she called it. When she'd named him that, it meant nothing to me, but now it meant something. I was waiting to see what. I bent down and kissed him on the nose and said, "Good-bye, little guy."

Mom had so much stuff in the car that I had to carry a poinsettia in my lap all the way home, but it did put me in a Christmassy mood, especially when she told me that after Barbie was finished with her lesson, we would start making spritz cookies, which were my favorite kind, and then ginger-bread men, which were Danny's favorites.

When Barbie got to our place, she kissed me on the cheek and wished me happy spring, because the shortest day of the year had come and gone and we had survived. She was in a good mood. As something to do during vacation, she and Alexis had asked if they could repaint their bathroom, and her mother had agreed, so as she told me while we were getting Blue out of the pasture (and she did pause to pet Gee Whiz, who nuzzled her hand), they had agreed to paint a picket fence around the whole bathroom. On each wall, above the picket fence, there would be a different scene. Barbie was to do two walls, one long and one short, and Alexis the other two. They were choosing their scenes independently, and Barbie felt that she had been inspired by the winter solstice. One of her walls, the one that faced south, would have a red, distant sun just peeping above the horizon, and lots of beautiful red, orange, pink, and yellow strips and ribbons of clouds. She hadn't de-cided on the other picture, but she did not want to do the ob-vious (summer solstice), especially as that wall looked east. Then we talked about the party. I said I'd liked Marie. Barbie said Marie had left for her ski trip. We agreed that Marie was "exotic."

I decided to do something that I'd never done with Barbie before, which was to get on another horse (in this case, Lin-coln) and ride with her while giving her her lesson. We mounted up outside the barn, and walked the horses over to the arena in a relaxed way. I didn't correct much of what she was doing—she was pretty beyond that now. In the arena, we walked around, practicing good manners—when we were abreast, we kept going and didn't let the horses argue. When she went ahead on Blue, I stayed three paces behind her, then passed her. When I was in the lead, I sped Lincoln up and slowed him down, and she had to watch me, and make sure that Blue kept the proper distance. We did an exercise where she passed me, then I passed her, then she passed me, all the way down the center line, at both the walk and the trot, then we trotted abreast in a circle and a figure eight, and finally, we cantered abreast, both directions. Lincoln was actually a little harder to handle than Blue, but that was because he wasn't as supple as Blue. When we were finished, I let her do her favorite thing, which was to canter around a few times at a pretty good clip, but I did not let her do it without the hard hat, which she wanted to do so that her hair could blow around her in the breeze. Then we walked them out by taking them into the mare pasture and riding down to the creek, though not into it, because it was ten or twelve inches deep and running fairly fast. We didn't say much, except that I occasionally told her some little thing, like "Sit back going downhill" or "Watch out for the gopher hole." We saw Rusty across the creek, scouting the far hillside for something or other.

It's a fairly steep hill from the creek to the top of the mare pasture. We leaned forward, and the horses exerted themselves to make the climb, and as soon as we were in sight of the fence line, we heard a loud and demanding whinny. I said, "Did you tell Gee Whiz we were going to get him out and let him run around?"

She said, "I think he read my mind."

"He seems to do that."

"Just the look on his face is really smart."

"You think that?"

"I do. He looks like this guy at school. Ben Rufus. He's really tall, like 6'4", and he never says much, but he's always watching, and when the teachers actually call on him and make him say something, he gives the right answer as if he thought about it so long ago that it isn't at all important to him anymore—he's way past right answers and wrong answers. He's a little intimidating."

I tried to imagine someone being intimidating to a Goldman twin. It wasn't easy. "Where's he from?"

"Canada. Vancouver."

Gee Whiz was pressing his chest against the gate enough for the gate to push against the latch, and I saw right then how he had gotten out—I must have left the latch not quite pushed far enough into its slot, and so when he pressed against the gate, it slipped out, and then the gate opened. I saw that we needed a chain and a clip. I shooed him away from the gate. He trotted in a little circle with his tail up. We untacked Blue and Lincoln, and when we put Lincoln in the pasture, he snaked his head and pinned his ears at Gee Whiz, as if to say, "You are not such a big shot!" Then he and Blue trotted out to the middle of the pasture and found nice places to roll. When Barbie and I carried the tack to the barn, Gee Whiz whinnied again, as if to say, "Why do I have to keep reminding you?"

I took the halter that had come with him off the gate, and when I opened the gate, he practically shoved his head into it. I realized that I had never led him anywhere before, and he was a *racehorse*, but he walked along properly, except that his strides were so big that Barbie and I had to hurry to keep up with him. For safety's sake, I put him first in the training pen. Then I grabbed the flag that was resting against the gatepost and followed him in. He, of course, would not know any of Jem Jarrow's lessons, but if I shook the flag at him, he would stay to the outside, away from me. I went to the center of the pen, lifted the flag, and waved it, not to scare him, but to see what he would do. He stared at me, flicked his ears and his tail, then turned gracefully, and started trotting around the pen to the left. At first, his stride was even but normal, and he looked like a pleasant enough horse, though of course, gigantic. But after he'd made his way around the pen twice, maybe just to check out the space, he pricked his ears, lowered his head, and opened up. His stride was smooth, efficient, and huge, as rhythmic as a machine and, it appeared, perfectly natural—when I wanted Blue to speed up his trot (which was not his best gait), I could urge him, and he would do it, but when I stopped urging, he went back to his normal self, like a spring that has a certain natural bounce. Gee Whiz's natural bounce was much bigger. I called out, "Easy! Whoa!" and stepped toward his head, and he slowed down. He walked, paused for a moment, then realized that he was being asked to turn around. He did so. I waved the flag, and he took off again, his stride huge and mesmerizing. I just stood there with the flag at my side, and he went around until he felt like slowing to the walk. Then I saw that his walk, too, which I hadn't really noticed, other than seeing that he was crossing the pasture or investigating something, was also big and sinuous.

Barbie said, "He looks different from Tooter. Blue, too."

I said, "He's different from any horse I've seen, at least that I remember."

"He's really big."

"That's part of it." He stopped walking and turned to look at me. I went up to him, grabbed his halter, and walked him over to the fence. "I mean, look at his legs. They're really long." I stood right up beside his left foreleg and put the outside of my hand against his elbow. My thumb was at my rib cage.

Barbie said, "It's not just that they're long, it's that they're

127

long compared to the rest of him." And that was true, too. She said, "Let's take him into the arena."

"Okay, but we're not going to do anything to make him run around. We're just going to stand there and see what he does."

"Of course! It's a psychological test. Who is this mysterious stranger? What does he really want?"

"He for sure really wants something. He acts like that all the time." I snapped on the lead rope, and we led him over to the arena. The best psychological test, I thought, was not to let go of him at the gate but to lead him to the center, where he could go any direction he wanted, and see what he chose, so we did this. I took off the halter so that he would feel completely free. For about thirty seconds, all of us stood absolutely still. Gee Whiz looked at Barbie and me, then off into the distance, then at the barn, then away from the barn. Blue and Jack would have taken off trotting, then started galloping, but Gee Whiz didn't know this place, and so he started walking— sniffing the poles, sniffing the half-collapsed straw bales, sniffing the jump standards and the cones. Then he trotted away from us over toward the railing, and he seemed to investigate that, too. It was boring in a way, because he wasn't doing anything exciting, but Barbie said, "What he really wants is to find out." This seemed to be true. Even when there weren't particular objects he was sniffing and looking at, there were perspectives—he wanted to see what his new home looked like from the arena, and how it was different from what it looked like from the pasture. Only when he was finished exploring did he start moving, first at the trot—that huge trot once again—and then, gathering and lifting himself, at the canter. He cantered, but not in a straight line—he turned and switched leads and made loops and crossed the center. It was an easy and supple canter, not rocking and delightful, like Blue's, but useful—to him. It was Gee Whiz's own canter, and he could do whatever he wanted while cantering. It was not about being ridden, but about doing what he wanted to do.

And then he opened up and started to gallop.

Now he went in a straight line, keeping to the outside of the arena. It reminded me immediately of Blue and Jack's little race, which I'd never happened to mention to anyone, except that however enjoyable it was to watch Blue and Jack, this was different. This horse was a professional, and his gallop was powerful and directed in a way that neither of them could understand. His stride was huge and flat, and his legs were like precision instruments in the way they touched the ground, then folded, then stretched. It was also clear from his expression that he was no longer exploring, that now he was galloping for the fun of it. Barbie and I stood there watching him (and I glanced at her—her eyes were wide and her mouth was hanging open, which made me laugh). And just as though he knew what he was doing, he made a loop at the end of the arena and went back the other way. Only now did he kick up.

I said, "They say that the gallop and the canter are actually different gaits, but I never saw that before now."

She said, "Can I never do that? Can I never go that fast?"

I knew what she meant. But I wasn't sure I *never* wanted to do it.

We watched him gallop five times around the arena. For

about three of them, he was full out, then he slowed some-what, but he was still moving at a fast pace. Then he broke to the trot and trotted once around, then he came down to the walk and took several deep breaths, blew the air out of his nostrils, and shook his head. We were still standing in the center of the arena. When we stepped toward him, he came toward us. I said, "I forgot the carrot!"

Barbie pulled her hand out of her pocket. She had two sugar lumps. I said, "Just give him one."

He came and took it and walked away. He went back to strolling along, checking out the arena and the views. Barbie said, "Should I walk him?"

"I don't think you have to lead him, but you can walk along near him and cluck if he stops walking. That should keep him going." She did this, every so often walking up to him and giving him a pat, but not trying to catch him. As for me, I built a jumping chute.

Yes, he had galloped himself breathless, but he was in good shape, and he caught his wind after four or five minutes. He was still alert and active, and didn't look at all tired. Maybe two weeks before, he had run a race, so he was well conditioned.

The jumping chute was along the railing, only one jump with a chute made of three poles to one side and three poles to the other side. The "jump" was three poles also, in a little pyramid, two poles on the ground and one pole resting on them. Altogether, the jump was maybe four or five inches high. While I was setting the poles, Gee Whiz came over and watched me for a moment, and then sniffed the poles. I stepped over them. He stepped over them. I turned around and stepped over them. He turned around and stepped over them. Barbie shouted, "Yay!"

He didn't mind going down the chute, even though all I had to give him was tufts of green grass. But Barbie would hold him at one end, and I would trot down over the poles, then shout, "Gee Whiz!" He would trot to me over the poles, and I would say, "Yup!" like Ralph Carmichael, and give him the grass. He ate up the grass like sugar.

Then I made a real jump, maybe a foot. He snorted the first time and looked at it, but he did jump it, and the second time and the third time he cantered to it, bent his knees, lifted his shoulders, and went. I gave him some grass, led him back to Barbie, and said, "Okay, one more time." She held him there while I walked to my end.

I called, "Okay, let him go!"

She let go.

I called, "Gee Whiz!"

He trotted toward me, then picked up the canter. But when he was about three strides out from the little fence, a crow flew off the railing of the arena, right at him. He threw his head, shifted his weight to the left, turned. And then he jumped the chute itself, which must have been three feet or 3'3", in perfect form, even though he was at an angle. He landed neatly on his right lead, made a half circle around the rest of the chute, and stopped in front of me. I said, "Yup!" and gave him the grass.

Barbie came running over. She was wide-eyed. She said, "I thought he was going to run right over you!"

"That occurred to me, but Dad says if they're coming at you, stand absolutely still so they know where to stop."

"He knew where to stop."

"I wasn't actually nervous, because he wasn't afraid. He looked like he knew what he was doing."

"I love him!" said Barbie. "Whose horse is he?"

I said, "I don't know."

But I thought I knew what his next career was going to be—he had been spooked, seen the jump, and jumped it perfectly, all in about one stride. Not every horse could or would do that. We petted him, and then Barbie walked him around while I put away the poles and the standards. When her mom showed up and my mom went outside to chat, both of them asked us what we'd been doing, and I said, "Oh, just this and that." I thought I would get around to telling about Gee Whiz's adventure at the supper table, when everyone was eating and in a good mood. Because I really didn't know whose horse he was.

Sawcow

Mounting Block

Chapter 8

I was ready for the weekend to be all Christmas. After Barbie left, I went upstairs to change clothes and wash up. When I came down, the cookie factory was set up. The dough was made. We buttered the pans, and then Mom's job was to press out the little trees, the little snowflakes, the little stars, the little wreaths. My job was the sprinkles. When the sprinkles were on, we put them in the oven, and started on another set of pans—Mom had lots of pans. After not very long, the kitchen table was covered with baked cookies cooling, and Mom was getting out the cookie cutters for the gingerbread men. This dough was made also—it had been chilling all day, and once she got it out, she had to work fast to roll it and cut it. My job was to butter the pans, put red hots on the gingerbread men for eyes and a row of buttons down the front, and then take a spatula and very carefully put the little men onto the pans. While the gingerbread men were baking, we put the spritz cookies in boxes for the brothers and sisters, and then, after the gingerbread men had cooled, we set a few of them in each box as well.

Always on the twenty-third of December, Mom had us eat leftovers so that there would be plenty of room in the refrigerator once she started cooking, both for church on the twenty-fourth (turkey and stuffing) and for our own Christmas dinner on the twenty-fifth (Danny was coming, so she was planning pot roast and pecan pie). Some of the leftovers were from the back of the refrigerator—old meat loaf, a wrinkled baked potato, nine string beans, two pieces of fried chicken (a wing and a leg), six Brussels sprouts, stuff like that, but we did get to finish the apple pie, because she needed the pie plate. After dinner, we washed all the dishes and set out the pots and pans she would need to start cooking, and Dad even defrosted the freezer, which he hadn't done in six months. I brought my stereo down from my room and set it on a table in the living room, right outside the kitchen doorway, and we put on an album of Christmas carols. Mom and Dad sang along, and I did, too, once in a while. In the meantime, Dad was breaking ice out of the freezer, the water was running in the sink, dishes were clattering, and the teakettle on the stove was whistling, because Dad was using hot water to help his defrosting. The only thing we could hear was ourselves, until the record came to an end and Mom realized that Rusty was barking.

As a rule, Rusty was a quiet dog. She had her business keeping an eye on things, and she had her other business, following Mom around, hoping for a scratch around the ears or a stray scrap. She had done some pretty amazing things—bring us a kitten, chase away coyotes, kill a young bobcat that was in the horse pasture—but she almost never barked while performing them. So when we heard her barking and barking and barking, all three of us stopped what we were doing and listened. Dad said, "It sounds as though she's out back."

I opened the back door.

There were horses everywhere.

Dad turned on the porch light, but that made it hard to see into the yard, so he turned it off again. We could hear Rusty barking out in the dark somewhere. And then my eyes adjusted. Blue and Lady were the nearest. They were about ten feet from the porch, nosing the ground for bits of leaves or grass. They looked up when I said their names. Behind Blue was a dark-colored horse, who I realized was Lincoln, and not far from Lincoln, maybe halfway to the barn, was Marcus, who snorted when Dad went down the steps. Very dimly, off in the distance, I could recognize Oh My from her white parts. Gee Whiz was standing behind her, also white in the starlight (the moon hadn't risen yet). Dad moved smoothly over toward Marcus, who snorted and backed up, but let himself be caught. Dad took hold of his forelock, then eased a piece of baling twine out of his pocket and wrapped it around Marcus's muzzle and his poll as a makeshift halter. He then led him back toward the barn. I had no trouble catching Blue—he just followed me—while Mom used a twisted dish towel around Lady's neck to lead her. At the barn, we put those three horses in stalls.

Rusty had prevented Nobby and Morning Glory from

getting out—she was sitting in the gate opening, barking at them. They were staying far from the gate, but Rusty seemed to think they would storm her if she gave them the chance, and it is true that horses like to be with the other members of their herd. Dad ran to the gate and closed it, and Rusty stopped barking. Then we took some halters and approached Gee Whiz and Oh My. They curvetted away from us and trotted off. I stood still—it wouldn't work to chase them—and Dad went into the barn. He came out with two little buckets, and he was already shaking them to show the horses that he had some oats. I wasn't sure it would work—they had gotten their hay only a couple of hours before, so I didn't think they were hungry. However, oats were always interesting, since they were sweet and the horses didn't get many oats (the sleek ones didn't get any oats). I didn't see Beebop anywhere, but he was a dark-colored horse with no white markings. I told myself not to worry, at least until the current problem had been taken care of.

Gee Whiz had been on the far side of Oh My, but while we were doing things, he'd come around so that he was between us and her. When Dad said, "Come on, kiddos, look at this," and shook the bucket, I could swear that I saw Oh My's ears prick ("Oats!") and then Gee Whiz coil his neck and nip her on the shoulder, pushing her back. Dad stopped moving. Gee Whiz was maybe twenty feet away, looking at us, his head pale, his eyes dark, his ears flicking.

I said, "I don't think he's going to let us catch him. I think he's got to come to us."

Dad let out a fed-up sort of sigh, but nothing that might excite the two horses. Mom said, "Apples? Carrots? Cookies?"

Dad said, "Do you have any apples? Those are the most fragrant."

"There are some in the larder."

"Well, go in and cut a couple into pieces and sprinkle on some sugar to make them juice up. If they can resist that, then they are superhorses."

Mom went inside, and Dad stood quietly, shaking the oats. I did what Jem Jarrow would have suggested—I half turned so that I was looking away from the horses. Sometimes they're more likely to come if you aren't confronting them. Jack, for example, always wanted to know what I was doing if I was paying attention to something other than him.

Mom came out with the pie plate heaped with apple chunks and brought them over to Dad. Dad said, "Give them to Abby. She's spent more time with him than we have."

I took the pie plate and lifted it toward my nose, and said, "Mmm. Those smell good." And they did, fresh and tangy. I rattled them around in the plate. Gee Whiz snorted and Oh My stuck her nose out underneath his neck. Without moving toward her, I held one out to her, and I think she would have taken it if he hadn't bumped her with his shoulder and pushed her away. She certainly didn't like it—she pinned her ears at him—but she also didn't come for the apple. I took one small step toward them.

Mom said, "Eat one."

I picked a piece up and made a big deal of putting it in my mouth, then slurping it down. Gee Whiz's nostrils twitched. But when Dad shifted position, Gee Whiz backed away. Mom said, "Let Abby do it. I think he likes her."

Dad set his bucket down where the horses could see it and

moved away. I stood quietly, only occasionally shaking the pan, not for the sound, but for the fragrance—horses have good noses, and they use them a lot, not only for deciding which little plants to eat, but also for deciding who their friends are, and what other horses are up to. They sniff noses when they meet and only then offer to be friends or enemies. Uncle Luke said a horse could find his way home with his sense of smell—if the wind was blowing from home to the horse—but I had never seen that. However, the breeze was blowing, gently, from me to Gee Whiz and Oh My, and if I could smell the apples, they could, too. I could see by the look on his face that Gee Whiz was making up his mind, and furthermore, that Oh My had already made up hers—she wanted some apples, and maybe some oats, and probably to go back into her pasture with her friends—but he wasn't going to make it easy for her. He pushed her again, and nipped her, and she jumped out of the way. Then she trotted off, and he spun around and went after her. I shouted, "Oh My! Oh My!" and shook the pan. She pivoted to avoid him, kicked out at him, and came trotting up. As she did, he came after her, but Dad jumped out at him and waved the halter and lead rope in his face. He backed up, and I caught Oh My and gave her about half of the apples. Dad slipped the halter on her and led her into the barn. Now it was just us and Gee Whiz. He kept snorting, so Dad and Mom sort of faded away, and it was just me and Gee Whiz.

I turned and walked away from him, slowly and ostenta-tiously leaning down and picking tufts of grass and putting them in the plate with the apples. I told myself that I didn't care whether he came or not—after all, he couldn't get out of the property, because the big gate was closed, and so what if he ate a few marigolds and some rosebushes and the grass in the front yard. I took some deep breaths. I did this because he reminded me of some of the boys at school—as soon as someone told them what they were supposed to do, well, that was exactly the last thing that those boys would do. Why they were that way, I had no idea, and Dad would have said that horses aren't people, and it's always the carrot or the stick, but sometimes the carrot didn't work, and maybe that was because the horse really was reading your mind. When the plate was full of nice, moist grass and sugared apple chunks, I set it on the mounting block near the barn and walked away from it (not forgetting to take a few apple chunks with me).

Gee Whiz waited maybe two minutes after I walked away, and then he walked toward the plate, sniffed it, and ate what was on it. While he was doing that, I moved slowly toward him, holding out an apple chunk. When he took it, I turned and walked away. After several very long seconds, he followed me. I walked. He walked. I halted. He walked a step or two. I walked. He walked. I halted. He came up to me. I gave him an apple chunk and walked away. Now I had one left. At this point, we were about halfway between the house and the barn. I could see Dad and Mom looking out the kitchen window. I went back to the mounting block and sat down on it and pretended to be minding my own business. I did have a rope with me, but not a halter.

I sat there.

It was breezy and cold. I bent my knees and wrapped my arms around them.

Gee Whiz came up to me and nuzzled me.

I ignored him.

He nuzzled me again.

I said, "Yup!" and while he was eating the apple chunk, I slipped the rope around his neck. I sat up, and he didn't pull away. I petted him down the neck and tickled him under the forelock while he sniffed me for more apples. Finally, I got to my feet and led him into the barn. He didn't pull away. I put him in a stall.

All the other horses were staring at him. I would have liked to know what they were thinking.

Beebop turned out to be in the front yard, which made perfect sense, since that's where the good grass was.

We put the horses back in their respective pastures, and when Dad walked away, I looked as best I could at the latch of the mare pasture. It was in much better shape than the latch of the gelding pasture—the slot that the bolt shot into was deep, and the bolt moved more easily. If a horse leaned on the gate, nothing would happen. But maybe it worked too well. Maybe a smart horse could take the handle of the latch between his lips and slide it back. He wouldn't have to then open the gate—any mare who leaned against it would push it open. I then went to look at the gelding latch. I had been the last one to close the gate, after Barbie and I put Gee Whiz away. I remembered making sure to push the bolt as far into the slot as I could, and I had then tried it. It seemed secure to me.

The geldings had walked deep into the pasture—farther than I could see them, but I could hear them moving around under the trees. I took one of the lead ropes and tied it around the gate and the post, making a square knot. Rusty was sitting on the porch when I got there, and I talked to her while I slipped off my boots. I said, "You know what happened, don't you? You know everything that happens, but we can never get you to tell us a thing." I patted her on the head.

Back in the house, we went on with Christmas preparations. I could see that Dad was annoyed, but he didn't say anything, only that I'd done a good job catching the horse, and thank the Lord. I just said, "Maybe I didn't work the latch properly and they pushed the gate open or something. I tied a rope around it for tonight."

Dad said, "I have been meaning to whittle that out a little." Mom kissed me on the cheek. Pretty soon, everything was clean and it was time for bed.

We put the Christmas tree up in the morning—no riding. Dad liked to put the Christmas tree up on Christmas Eve and take it down on New Year's Day so that we "wouldn't get tired of the celebration of the birth of the Lord." When we got to church before four, everyone was there—Sister Brooks had brought Brother Abner, and even Ezra Brooks, who never said anything, was sitting in his usual seat in the back of the room. We were all wearing nice clothes. I was wearing the black-and-white dress Mom had bought me when we were looking for school clothes, plus a black satin headband and pumps. I thought I looked pretty good, and Carlie Hollingsworth did, too—she said, "Oh, that look is so sophisticated!" Carlie's dress was bright red, and she had a sprig of holly pinned to her shoulder. She looked like she should be in a department-store window. Mom wore her best navy-blue dress and she also had a corsage—a beautiful white gardenia that smelled like heaven. Dad had on his favorite shirt, his best boots, and black trousers that weren't jeans.

Sister Larkin was already setting up the candles—a hundred of them—and everyone helped her. Then we set out the food for an early supper. Mom had taken the turkey out of the oven just as we left the house so that it would have its required rest on the way to church. While Dad carved it, the other brothers and sisters put out what they had made, and it was quite a feast—shrimp with cocktail sauce, mashed potatoes, sweet potatoes with marshmallows, three or four vegetable casseroles, two kinds of rolls, Mom's pie, Sister Brooks's pie (pumpkin), cupcakes frosted in red and green. I was glad to see there was no Jell-O. Once it was all set out, Mr. Hollingsworth got out his camera and took a picture, then we helped ourselves. I watched Carlie—she took small helpings of everything. I did, too (though a little extra of the turkey and the shrimp), because that's what wearing a nice dress does to you. I also took three napkins.

At exactly six o'clock, even though some people were still eating their main course, Dad, Mr. Hollingsworth, and Brother Larrabee began lighting the candles. When they were all lit, one of the sisters turned off the lights. By this time, we'd finished with our food, and taken our plates to the table at the back of the room. Now we went to the front of the room and sang "O Come, O Come, Emmanuel," the first carol. We always sang six carols in a row that told the story of Jesus's birth—"O Come, O Come, Emmanuel" was about the Israelites wishing for the advent of their Savior, "The Cherry Tree Carol" was about Joseph and Mary going to Bethlehem (this one always made me cry for some reason), "Joy to the World" was about Jesus being born, "Angels We Have Heard on High" was about the angels announcing the birth, "Away in a Manger" was about Jesus waking up in his manger, and "We Three Kings" was about the three wise men arriving with their gifts. The brothers and sisters knew these carols as well as they knew their own names—they had been singing them, often together, for years, and they knew all the tunes and all the harmonies. Even when their voices were old and shaky, they knew how to make this music very pure and beautiful. I knew my parts, too—I had been singing them my whole life.

Everyone was smiling and pleased after the carols. We sat down and got comfortable. Brother Brooks stood up and opened his Bible to the first Christmas story, the one in Luke. Then Dad got up, and opened his Bible to Matthew, and read that one. The two stories are kind of different, and I preferred the Luke one, but Dad said that it was important to know, from Matthew, how hard it was for Jesus to find his place, and that hardship was often a gift, if you could get yourself to see it that way. However, Christmas wasn't a time when the brothers and the sisters looked in the Bible for advice and guidance—they just read the passages and celebrated what happened. After the reading, we sang more carols—"It Came Upon a Midnight Clear," "O Come, All Ye Faithful," "I Heard the Bells on Christmas Day," and "The Twelve Days of Christmas." Then Sister Larrabee, who had a beautiful voice and had once sung in a professional choir, stood up and sang "Lo, How a Rose E're Blooming," which I thought was the most beautiful. After she was finished and sat down, everyone was silent for a while, and most people bent their heads. I prayed for Danny first of all, and then for all the horses.

After we prayed silently, Mr. Hollingsworth got up and said a long prayer for all of us, that we should ask the Lord for his help in avoiding temptation, in loving our friends and our enemies, in knowing what was right, in facing up to trials with strength and joy, in following the path of Jesus in everything we did. He thanked the Lord for his word, which we could turn to anytime we felt we had to or wanted to. He kissed his Bible, and sat down. We all said, "Amen!" Right next to me, Dad let out one of his grunts—he didn't like anyone kissing the Bible, because that made it into an idol. But he didn't say anything. He had pretty much learned to keep his opinions to himself.

Now there was dessert. Mom and Mrs. Hollingsworth cut the pies into small slices, and set one of each onto every plate, along with a cookie. Carlie and I carried the plates to each of the brothers and sisters, and Erica Hollingsworth handed out napkins and forks. Some of the brothers and sisters started chatting about Christmas treats when they were children— mincemeat pie, which had raisins, apples, and candied orange peel, but also suet and minced beef. It made me gag to think of it. Then someone remembered plum pudding, which had not only suet, but also treacle, brandy, and beer. Brother

Abner remembered something called a clootie pudding, which was made with bread crumbs, raisins, and currants. It was full of spices, and even though his mother had a range in her kitchen, she liked to steam it, then dry it in the traditional way, by hanging it in a bag near an open fire. He said, "Half the time she was in the kitchen making Christmas supper, she had to run out and stop us boys from hitting the clootie with a stick to make it swing. Ah, it was so tempting." He laughed.

One of the sisters said, "Brother Abner, I don't believe half the tales you tell about your family—you couldn't have been as wild as you say."

"Oh, wilder than that!" said Brother Abner. "Four boys in five years is more than any mother can handle. My brother Jacob went to sea when he was thirteen. That was 1888. And we didn't live anywhere near the ocean. But he had a passion to do it, and one day, he just walked away. My mother was frantic, but my father said he would turn up, and sure enough, he did. After a week, we got a letter from him saying that he'd got himself a position as a cabin boy on a merchant ship sailing to Brazil. I didn't even know what Brazil was, and maybe he didn't, either. I went there eventually. Not like any other place I've ever been."

I saw that the sisters were glancing at one another, and then Mom said, "Did you ever see the Amazon River?"

"Oh, I did. Went up the river as far as Macapá, which isn't all that far, maybe the same as from New Orleans to Baton Rouge, on the Mississippi, but you can only get there by boat. River's huge around there. Mostly in Brazil I worked on a rubber plantation. You could do that in those days—did that in Malaya, too. In Hawaii, I worked on a sugar plantation. Just kicked around the world a little too long, I've got to say."

Carlie said, "What was your favorite place?"

Brother Abner gave a big smile as he looked at her, then he said, "Well, in order to decide that, you got to choose between which place was the strangest, or which place was the most beautiful, or in which place were you the happiest? The three aren't often the same."

Mom said, "I want to hear all three."

"Well . . . ," said Brother Abner. Then he coughed, wiped his mouth, and took a little drink of water.

"Maybe everyone says that the most beautiful is Paris, and Paris is a wonderful town, but I thought the most beautiful spot was on an island in the Caribbean, down from Florida a good ways, called St. Thomas. A white sand bay like you've never seen anywhere else. Sir Francis Drake used to lie in wait for pirate ships there. It's not a place to live in, but it is beautiful. I guess for strangest, that would be Istanbul, it is now. It used to be Constantinople."

"Constantinople, can you spell it?" muttered Erica. The answer to that question was "i-t." That was all we knew about Constantinople.

Brother Abner said, "Well, you see, Istanbul connects two continents, Asia and Europe, and you can see that right there, when you're walking around, in everything that they do. Part of the city looks west and part of the city looks east and part of the city looks back and part of the city looks forward. I just couldn't get enough when I was there. There are bits from

Roman times, and there's a huge museum there called Hagia Sophia that was a cathedral, then a mosque. Biggest church in the world, for a while. Looking at it makes you feel like the Romans and the sultans are just around the corner, if you could only manage to see them. Then there's another mosque, too, they call the Blue Mosque, all blue tiles inside. Then there's the Grand Bazaar, which is a huge market full of shops, and every shop is overflowing with things. Across the straits, it's all different, somehow. I couldn't get enough of walking around there."

Mom took Brother Abner's hand and said, "Was that where you were happiest?"

"Oh my, no," said Brother Abner. "Never could fit in there. Too sunny and busy for a fellow from way upstate New York, USA!" He laughed. "I was happy in Seattle. I had some friends there. We had a little money, enough to feel safe and comfortable from day to day. Good friends. Good food. Thought it would last forever, like you do. But in some ways, the memory is good enough. Out on the flats in the eelgrass, laughing and looking for crabs. Or just walking around town in the evening, thinking it was going to rain forever." He laughed again. "You got good friends, even the rain is fine with you."

I said, "I would like to see some of those places."

And Brother Abner said, "Miss Abby, nothing is stopping you."

After that, everyone got to talking about other things, and I looked for a while at Brother Abner. He looked better than he had the week before, and the sisters were not whispering about him. As Mom would have said, his color was pretty good and he seemed "spry." I guess Mr. Hollingsworth had had his Studebaker towed to the repair shop, and they were going to fix it after Christmas, and until then, he had agreed that the sisters could look in on him every day. He had his plate in his lap. He'd eaten the pumpkin pie and part of the cupcake.

Mom lifted her eyebrows at me, and I poked Carlie. We got up and went around, taking the plates and forks and putting them with the other dirty dishes in the back of the room.

We were used to sitting in church maybe five hours every Sunday—service, then lunch, then Sunday school—but that started by ten in the morning. Now we'd only been there maybe two hours, but everyone was yawning, and Sister Brooks went around and snuffed the candles with a brass candlesnuffer. We all watched her quietly when she did this— that was the end of the candlelight service for another year. Cleaning up took quite a while—partly because the sisters divided up the leftovers for some of the ones who weren't going to have another Christmas dinner, including Brother Abner. Mom also handed out her little boxes of cookies. Sister Larrabee gave me a secret present, which I opened when I got home—it turned out to be a knitted hat with matching mittens. They were cute—she had knitted a horse into the hat and into the back of each of the mittens. She was a very good knitter who didn't have so many people to knit for.

On the way home, Mom was yawning, and Dad was quiet, so I knew he might be pretty tired, too, especially since we still had to check the horses and give them some more hay. I was also tired, so I was really hoping that Gee Whiz did not

150

know how to untie knots. To make myself stop thinking about this, I said, "How do you think Brother Abner joined our church?" He had been there as long as I could remember.

"I don't know about that," said Mom. "He was here when we came."

"He told me once," said Dad. "He was raised Methodist, but fell away when he left home. Then, down in Australia, I think, during the war, oh goodness, he would have been in his sixties by then, he was just walking down the street, and a man stepped up to him, and something about the man struck him, and when the man said he had something to tell Brother Abner, Brother Abner listened—'For once, I listened,' he said to me. 'Can't say I ever listened to a thing before that. I was a contrary fellow for most of my life.' I guess when he got back around here after the war, he found Sister Brooks's uncle, and helped him start up the church."

I said, "I'd like to ask him about Australia."

They didn't say anything.

The horses were quiet as little mice in their pastures when we got home, and Rusty was curled up, sleeping in her bed on the back porch.

Danny was already there when we got up in the morning, and, merry Christmas, he had already fed the horses, so we didn't have to get out of our pajamas. Mom went straight into the kitchen and made pancake batter, and I turned on the Christmas tree and lay down on the rug under it and stared up through the boughs. I could see all the ornaments we'd made or bought over the years, and the ones that our grandparents had sent us—the crocheted snowflakes from my mom's

grandmother were the most beautiful; there were four of them,
a different one every year, white and lacy, and of course, no
two alike. One year, Mom had baked fake gingerbread men,
not for eating, and we'd decorated those and hung them with
little green ribbons. One year, Danny and I had strung what
seemed like an endless string of popcorn and cranberries—we
still had that, too. There was also a string of lights that looked
like candles—they bubbled. Mom did not like them because
they got very hot, so she only let them be plugged in when
someone was in the room. But they sat up on the branches
and were very pretty.

Dad had decided not to sell Oh My, or any other horse—
not even Morning Glory—until the spring, when he thought
they would be better trained and we could get a good price for
them, so we knew there wouldn't be many presents. Mom
bought me a sweater set—a blue pullover and cardigan to go,
she said, with my eyes. Dad gave me a shirt, red with yellow
piping and a sunflower embroidered on the back. I'd bought
Mom's present months before, a pair of sheepskin slippers,
and I gave Dad a new riata, which Danny helped me pick out,
for roping those calves that might come, or at least for roping
the sawcow. It was Danny who gave the big presents—to
Mom, a cashmere jacket (Leah had helped him pick it out in
San Francisco); to Dad, a new pair of chaps with his initials
tooled into them; and to me, a hard hat, gloves, and a whip
for showing, along with a book called *Horsemanship*, by a man
named Waldemar Seunig. I opened it to the first page, and
read, "Books do not make a rider good or bad, but they can
make him better or worse." Danny's presents made me a little
sad, because I knew they might be good-bye presents.

There was also a gift under the tree, wrapped with a bow and a tag, for Gee Whiz. I opened it. It was from Santa, and was a chain with a clip on the end. I realized that Leah must have repeated to Danny what I'd said at the slumber party about Gee Whiz's escape. We all laughed, but it was Christmas, and no one said anything more about it. Anyway, his board was paid for a month, and that wouldn't end until January fifteenth.

Since Christmas lasted all day, and there wasn't much to do, I did read the book a little. It was not like any book I'd read, even the cavalry manual with the drawings that looked like Blue that I'd read in the early fall. Some sentences made me laugh, especially ones about buying a horse and discovering that "his horse will never again travel as well, despite correct training . . . , as it did on that bright autumn morning on the imperceptibly rising show track in the castle park," and I realized this was true—when a horse trots slightly uphill, he always looks brighter and better. But I got lost in the words and the pictures—the Spanish Riding School, medium trot, levade, capriole, extended walk, equestrian poise, engaged, two tracks. Here I thought I knew what I was doing, at least in a way, and I didn't know what in the world Waldemar Seunig was talking about. I couldn't even pronounce his name. There was one picture I stared at for a long time—a man on a horse in the Pan American Games, sliding down a hill to a jump at the bottom. A man on a horse is pretty tall, say, eight feet tall. In this picture, the man and the horse were lost against what looked like the face of a cliff. There were plenty of pictures of men (and a woman, too) riding and jumping high jumps.

When Danny and I went out to give the horses their

evening hay (I was out of my pajamas by this time, but still yawning), I told him about Gee Whiz's little session with Barbie and me, how he seemed to enjoy himself, and how, when he had to, he jumped over a 3'3" jump at an angle, and easily. It was dark, and if the days were lengthening, I couldn't tell. We'd already eaten our pie. Danny was supposed to leave after we finished with the hay, and I was sure he was going out with Leah. He didn't say anything, just threw the hay. Gee Whiz was dimly visible at the far end of the pasture, looking up the hill. When he saw us, he did whinny and trot over to where we usually threw his pile. After we put out the hay, I hooked the chain around the gate and the gatepost, and clipped the two ends tightly together.

Finally, Danny said, "Ike told me all about him, more than Ross did. For one thing, he was born in France, and imported to the US as a yearling. I don't know why they would bring him over, except that he was a really good-looking yearling. His auction price at Saratoga was a hundred thousand dollars."

"Where is Saratoga?"

"New York somewhere. It's a big resort town with a race-track from the old days. They have a huge yearling auction, and then the horses sometimes go into training, and sometimes wait for a while. Man o' War raced there. He also lost his only race there because he was facing the wrong direction when they started, according to Ike. Anyway, Gee Whiz ran there as a two-year-old and won two races, then he won a big race in Florida as a three-year-old, and they really thought they had something. He was second in the Arkansas Derby, and that was where he bowed a tendon, so he was out. Ike said maybe he was too big—sometimes when they grow fast, racing as a three-year-old is extra hard on them. Anyway, he was always sound after he came back the summer he was four, and always game. I don't see how, just because he had a little bad luck, he doesn't still have that ability. Lots of ex-racehorses make great riding horses."

"He's so big."

"But he carries it well. He's perfectly constructed. Even the angle of his pasterns and the shape of his hooves are perfect. Even the shape of his ears is perfect."

I said, "You bought him, didn't you?"

Danny began pushing the wheelbarrow back to the barn. "Roscoe gave him to me."

I ran after him. "Danny! You might not even be here to train him!"

He stopped and stared at me. "Something to come home to, then."

Okay, I was shocked. It was one thing for Danny to buy Happy from Dad; Happy was a horse with scads of cow in her who would always be useful, and anyway, one who Dad loved—I'd overheard Dad saying that "whatever happens," Happy was fine at our place "for the duration." It was quite another thing to take on this very large and mysterious animal who, as far as Dad was concerned, didn't know a cow from a car. And who had already made one mess (only one, as far as Dad knew).

"Why can't someone else take him?"

"Because he's too good for that. You never know where he'll end up."

Meaning, I knew, slaughter.

I said, "You better start riding him, then."

And Danny said, "I will if you will."

I stared at him again. Then I said, "He's way too big for me." I thought, "And way too smart."

He said, "After my physical, I heard there would be three or four weeks. We can work on it." Then he said, "He likes you."

As if to underline this remark, Gee Whiz looked up from his hay and nickered.

Danny put the wheelbarrow away, washed his hands in the tack-room sink, and dried them on one of the towels there. Then he smoothed back his hair and said, "How do I look?"

"Like an idiot."

"Perfect." He poked me in the ribs, and then ran toward his car.

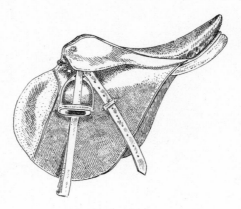

English Saddle

Western Saddle

Chapter 9

THE NEXT MORNING, CHRISTMAS WAS OVER, AND I WASN'T sad. Christmas is like a spell where everything moves extra slow and you try to remember what there is to do with your time. It's great to look forward to, but nicer to remember than to live through. We got up, got dressed in the almost dark, and went out and did our jobs. I made my riding plan, and Dad decided when to take Blue to the stables. As far as Jane knew, Melinda would be ready for her lesson the next day, and why not Ellen having a lesson, too? Jane would teach them, at least the first time. My lesson could be later in the week, whenever Mom had time to take me out there. I called Barbie and told her about Blue going to the stables, and suggested that she watch me take my lesson with Jane. She was happy to agree. She had finished her winter solstice painting, but Alexis had finished both of hers and Barbie was still stuck for a subject.

"What are Alexis's paintings?"

"One is as if you were standing on a hill, looking west over the ocean, and seeing only the top of the fog with a few dark hilltops jutting through, and stars in the dark sky above. The other is a green hillside full of lupine."

"My mom would buy that. She loves lupine."

"I think I have to do something urban, but I don't know what."

"You don't look out on anything urban."

"We don't look out on the ocean, either. But I think you just gave me an idea."

Yes, I had. I could hear it in her voice.

All the way to the stables, Dad talked about rain. There had been rain, but not enough. Now he was worried. Three inches, or was it four inches? Maybe we did need rain, but everything was beautiful out to the stables, sunny and blue and green. I had a sweater on, but I took it off. Jane was in shirtsleeves. She met us in the parking lot, and stood with her hands on her hips while I unhooked the ramp and Dad let it down. We had let Blue travel loose in the trailer, which was something Dad liked to do, so he was facing us, standing as though he were waiting for his picture to be taken, already looking around. Jane said, "Blue!" He looked at her. He knew his name. I led him down the ramp, and we went over to Gallant Man's stall. Jane said, "We swaddled him in cotton and shipped him off. They put such a head guard on him! They didn't care for a moment that his head was a yard lower than the inside of the trailer. I don't know how he would have bumped his head."

I said, "And he's too smart to do that, anyway."

"Well," said Dad, "I wish him luck." Maybe he knew how much those people in Los Angeles had paid for our pony, but of course no one was telling a kid like me.

Dad didn't want to wait around for Ellen and Melinda to have their lessons, and I didn't really want to, either. If they didn't like Blue, I'd be disappointed, because maybe he wasn't as good as I thought he was, and if they did like him, well, what next? I told myself that Blue was here mostly for my lesson on Wednesday, and that Saturday we would take him home. We talked about rain all the way home, too, only this time we talked about those clouds Dad had seen to the west, and maybe that was fog, but it looked more like clouds, awfully far off the coast, though—well, anything was welcome. At home, I rode Lincoln and Lady, and read some more of my strange book—"Realizing that the horse's will is governed principally by feelings of pleasure or discomfort, he will influence that will by evoking pleasurable feelings, which he associates with certain actions of the horse as a chain of cause-and-effect ideas." I thought Jem Jarrow would agree with that.

For lunch, we had grilled cheese. Dad's had bacon in it. I was yawning when Dad said, "I need to go over to the Marble Ranch this afternoon. Can you come with me?"

What else did I have to do but take a nap? Really, when there was no school, the days got rather long. I said, "Why are you going there?"

"They have a couple of calves that might work out for a few weeks. Or I could send Lady over there and Danny could work her. I haven't decided. But she needs the work."

He drove past the Marble Ranch, though, and stopped at the Vista del Canada gate. I said, "What's going on?"

He was grinning. He said, "All I know is that your instructions are to go to the gate, push the buzzer, and say that you are meeting Danny."

"You aren't coming?"

"No, I really do have an appointment at the Marble Ranch. When you're done, Danny will bring you over there, and we'll head home."

I got out of the car and he drove off. I pushed the buzzer. I was asked if I had a car. No. Then I was to go over to a smaller gate and wait. I looked around, saw a little paved path, and followed it. That gate opened, and I went in. It was a cool day, a little cloudy, and you could see that in the next day or so, it was going to rain. But here, at Vista del Canada, it was going to be a sparkling, beautiful rain—perfect drops that land on all the green leaves and hang there before slipping into the murmuring river.

A car showed up as I was walking down the road—it had VISTA DEL CANADA painted on the side, and in it was Ike. He said, "Hey, Abby! Good t' see ya! That colt is somethin' else. Now you get in, and we'll drive back there. Dan is shoein' a two-year-old, almost done, but couldn't get away. I guess yer gonna see yer boy go for a little jog, or maybe somethin' more excitin', but he's comin' along real nice. Wayne's already makin' a futures book for his Derby run."

I said, "What's a futures book?"

"Ah, ya bet a year in advance, or more. Great odds, but the chances of the horse even gettin' t' the post are pretty slim."

We drove past the big hillside pasture. All the mares and soon-to-be yearlings were grazing happily.

I said, "Why do I get to see this after lunch? I thought all the horses worked in the morning."

"Well, they mostly do. But Wayne was a bit under the weather this mornin', so since it's a nice cool day, he decided ta get on his late, and Roscoe said better late than never, so here ya are."

When we pulled up near Danny, he was still leaning over the back foot of a chestnut, rasping the outside of the hoof. He looked up, let the hoof drop, and waved. I got out of the car. The person holding the horse was Mr. Pelham. He waved as he walked the horse back to its stall. Danny was putting away his tools.

Now Wayne came off the track with a dark bay, almost a black. He jumped down, and one of the other grooms took the horse while Ike was coming with Jack. It wasn't possible, but Jack looked bigger. It had only been a few days since I'd seen him, but he'd grown, and if not in size, then in muscle and education. He seemed to know what Wayne was going to do, and when Wayne did it—sprang onto him, twisted into the saddle, and picked up the reins—Jack walked out onto the track smoothly and easily. Wayne was taking no chances, though. He had his toes in the stirrups, and he was hunched over, gripping both reins with both hands, making a bridge across Jack's neck. The reins weren't tight and weren't loose. There was no one else on the track—they had finished in the morning, and since it was almost three, there was no one in the center, grazing, either. Besides Danny and me, only Encantado was watching. Roscoe Pelham came and stood next to us. He said, "He has good manners. These colts who live out with each other for a year and hardly see a human don't seem to know how to say please and thank you. Nice shoulder, too."

Jack looked catlike and leggy. Roscoe Pelham said, "His walking strides are big and easy and his overstep is pretty impressive—see how the prints of his back hooves in the sand are a foot in front of the prints of his front hooves? That means that he'll have a big gallop and lots of power from behind." Danny nodded. I just stared. They walked along beside the rail. Jack tossed his head once or twice, and then Wayne let him go up into a trot.

I knew Jack's trot as well as I knew anything in this world, but still it looked different with a rider. Danny said, "Look at that," and how could you help it? He sprang along the ground, eating it up. But it was more than that—it was that his legs were so graceful and quick. He hardly seemed to be touching down.

Roscoe Pelham said, "See how he's built? He's built like a suspension bridge. He's just so well knit together from his ears all down his neck and withers and back to his haunches and his tail. Look how his tail just flows out of his backbone. The rider means nothing to him."

They trotted all the way around the track once, and then

partway around. Just at the point where they were passing En-cantado's paddock, the stallion whinnied, and Jack rose into a canter—not with a rush, as if he were afraid of the stallion, but his usual let-me-see-what's-going-on-over-there sort of lope. Wayne let him go about twenty strides, then eased him back down to the trot. "No hurry," said Mr. Pelham. "Got to build up a little muscle before he runs in the Derby."

But I didn't want to think of that—racing and crowds and all those strange things I knew nothing about except for excit-ing words. It was enough for me to watch him stretching those long legs, and being a good boy. He finished the second cir-cuit at the trot, and then came down to the walk, and Wayne let him go along on a looser rein. Jack looked at this and looked at that. When he passed us, he was breathing a little bit—his nostrils were wide—but his sides weren't heaving or anything. Everything he had done was easy for him. His ears flopped a little, showing that he was happy and relaxed. He walked once around, and then Ike met him at the gate. Wayne jumped off, patted Jack on the shoulder, and said, "So far, so good," and laughed. Jack So Far.

Roscoe Pelham headed for his truck and I followed Ike and Jack over to the little walking ring. Once Ike untacked him and put his halter on, he gave me the lead rope, and I walked him. Ike said, "Half an hour and don't just laze around. Want him ta move out, and stretch a little. I'm gonna put him in his paddock for an hour after this, but we want him ta look at the stall and say, 'Hallelujah, I can get a rest and eat my supper.'"

"He's been out his whole life."

"That's why ya gotta take it slow. But they git ta like the rest, that's what I think. I had a filly, we put her on stall rest after she tore her check ligament. Well, she was sleek and shinin' and never seemed at all anxious the whole time, and then when the doc examined that check ligament a month later—no progress at all, and I said, 'Well, why should she get better when bein' injured is such a pleasure for her?'"

Jack and I marched around the circle. Once or twice he sniffed my pocket to see if I had a treat, but he wasn't pushy about it. Twice when Encantado whinnied, he lifted his head. Over in the two banks of stalls, the other horses were pulling bits of hay out of their haynets, and staring at us, just a little. When I passed Ike, who was soaping bridles, I said, "What does he do tomorrow?"

"Oh, same as t'day. He aluz does what he wants ta, he just hasta do it under saddle and with Wayne pointin' the way. We don't push 'em at this age. Y'okay here?"

I nodded. We kept walking. Jack stayed just behind me, as he had been taught to do, but I could feel his energy, his youth, and even (something new) a sort of power. In the chilly air, his body was warm, but not cuddly. Every so often, I looked at him, wondering if in eight years he would have that solid, self-assured look that Gee Whiz had—not only the look of a mature horse, but the look of a horse who has been around, figured out his job, seen crowds and excitement. And then I wondered if maybe I wasn't misinterpreting Gee Whiz's curiosity—maybe he wasn't saying, "What's over there?" Maybe he was saying, "What happened to all the fun?"

After a while, Ike finished his work and left, so Danny and

I put Jack in the paddock, and while Danny was raking the gravel just a little bit, I stood at Jack's gate and stroked his face and neck, up under his cowlick and down his cheeks. He let me, at least for a minute or two. I murmured, "They like you, big boy. They like you. But I love you."

On Wednesday, when I got to the stables at ten, Barbie was already there, and she was watching Sophia take a lesson with Colonel Hawkins on Pie in the Sky. I hadn't told Barbie much about everything that went on with Pie in the Sky and Sophia over the fall. Now, as I looked back on it, it seemed to me like I made a mountain out of a molehill (and who has ever seen a molehill, really?). But what happens is, you think about something and think about it and think about it, and it gets bigger and bigger, and there you are, you can't think about anything else. What was great about the Carmichaels was that they did everything differently from everyone else, and watching them sort of woke you up, and once you woke up, you could think about things in a new way. Even if you ended up doing things mostly the way you always had, thinking about the new way helped you understand it better. I could see that now with Sophia. Her form was still perfect, and she was still brave and determined, but her body was just a little looser, her hands were just a little lighter, and she talked more. When I'd seen her taking lessons from Colonel Hawkins before, she'd always followed orders and never said a word (or cracked a smile). Now, while I was walking over to the fence, she was saying, "Okay, can I do a kind of spiral? I could take the triple in-and-out, then the brush, then the turn inward to the oxer followed by that brush, then finish with a circle through the three jumps at the center of the arena."

The colonel said, "What would that accomplish?"

Sophia said, "Well, it would be fun, I've never done it, and I think it would make him pay attention."

The colonel put his hands on his hips and blew out some air, then said, "Well, maybe you're right. Go ahead and try it."

I wasn't sure that the colonel was used to taking suggestions—he was a colonel after all, and there were no generals around. I leaned on the railing beside Barbie and watched. The inward spiral would be to the left. Sophia turned Pie to the right, asked him to canter from the walk (which he did, beautifully—I remembered that rocking, balanced gait), and made an elegant circle. Then she asked for the flying change, went to the left, and headed down over the nine jumps. You would never get a course like this in a show—they always want you to turn different directions, change leads, et cetera, but it looked graceful, and it was not that easy for Pie to bend ever more tightly, shorten his stride, pay attention. After the last fence, Sophia loosened her reins and let him gallop off. He tossed his head and kicked up, but as if he was enjoying himself, not as if he was angry. Sophia, of course, just went with his motion. Barbie said, "Was that really good, or do I just not know anything?"

I opened my mouth, but behind us, Jane said, "It was really good."

I said, "I thought so, too."

The colonel called out, "Excellent!"

Sophia leaned forward and patted Pie on the neck, then grinned.

Barbie said, "Sophia is very interesting. 'Wheels within wheels,' is what my mom would say."

I glanced at Jane, whose eyebrows flicked upward. We were used to thinking of Sophia as a great rider and sometimes a riddle, but "very interesting"? That was a new idea.

Jane said, "Ready?"

Barbie and I turned, and I introduced them, then we walked over to where Rodney had Blue all tacked up. He nickered to me, and I patted his cheek, then gave him a lump of sugar. Rodney, of course, had bathed him, pulled his mane, and shaped his tail, which now floated behind him in a light puff. And his bridle was cleaned and oiled, and his saddle, too, since I was using one of Jane's, a German jumping saddle called a Stübben. Rodney gave me a leg up, and we walked to the arena, not the big arena where Sophia was cooling Pie out, but one of the faraway ones, at the edge of the trees. I said, "Now that Blue is here, I could take him down to the beach through the forest."

"You could," said Jane. "It's a beautiful trail."

"Who would I ride?" said Barbie.

"We have plenty," said Jane.

The arena had a few jumps in it, and was neatly groomed. Jane said, "You show me, Abby."

So, after walking for ten minutes and stepping over and backing once or twice to warm up, I put on a little performance—walk, trot, canter, circles, figure eights, all three gaits on a long rein, faster walk, shorter walk, animated trot, sitting trot, hand gallop, lead changes. Blue was his usual smooth and cooperative self. I felt him listening to me as he always did, and I knew that part of his problem when I was having trouble in the fall (I was reminded of this by looking at Sophia and Pie) was that, yes, he was listening to me, but I was talking gibberish—do this, no do that, no speed up, no slow down, no don't worry, no *worry*! If your horse wants to please you, then you have to know what you want him to be doing.

Now Jane set the jumps at about 2'9", two down the long side, two at an angle in the center. I trotted one of the angled ones, then went around the end of the arena and came back over the other angled one, then I did that again, and after that, I trotted the two down the long side, first one direction and then the other. Blue behaved himself very nicely. Now I picked up the canter and did a sort of flat figure eight: down the long side to the right, loop at the end, over the first angled jump, then over the first jump on the long side, but to the left, then a loop, back over the second angled jump and the second jump on the long side, then around the whole arena and back over the two jumps down the long side. Eight jumps with a lot of easy turns. Blue took them all in stride, literally, and did proper lead changes. It didn't feel electric and floating, the way it did with Pie in the Sky—it felt smooth and routine, no big deal. But for a nervous horse, that was a true accomplishment. I came down to the walk and let him go around on a loose rein. Here and there he glanced toward the trees and flicked his ears, but he was just curious, not nervous.

Barbie said, "I love him."

Jane said, "He is a good boy. He was perfect with Melinda and Ellen—he seemed to adapt very nicely to their different riding styles."

"What are their different riding styles?" said Barbie.

"The nervous and the pushy. But he stayed calm for Melinda, as if he wanted to take care of her, which doesn't surprise me, since he took care of his owner for a long time before he came here. And patient for Ellen, as if he wasn't taking her seriously. I think she could do backflips on him, and he would say, 'Oh, right. Backflips.' I was impressed."

"When can I have a lesson?" said Barbie.

"Tomorrow?" said Jane.

"Yes, but I've only ridden western. I would love to try this, though."

I, of course, had been eavesdropping on this whole conversation. I said, "She has a good seat and great balance. And a good sense of rhythm."

I walked away on Blue. I had not meant to encourage this. We moseyed along the far side of the arena. The other thing about the woods was that they smelled piney. The trees were hugely tall and close together, growing in a bed of brown pine needles that lay up against the bottoms of the trunks. They were also filled with birds that flew here and there, and sat up high and cheeped and muttered. There was a woodpecker on the trunk of one tree at the far end of the arena—he was stashing an acorn in a hole he or another woodpecker had made; the entire trunk of the tree was a pantry of holes filled with acorns. I saw Jane and Barbie hurry away, chatting, and I kept walking Blue.

Of course they came back, and Barbie was in riding clothes, with a hard hat. Jane had a room full of used breeches, boots, shirts, coats—some right out of old movies like *National Velvet*. I went over to the gate, and Jane said, "Why not just try it out? Even if you only have twenty minutes, that's enough to get a sense of how far along you are."

I jumped off.

I didn't mind seeing Barbie on Blue—she'd ridden him several times, anyway, but here I was seeing her on him in *this place*, where he didn't have the air of being my horse, where horses of all kinds came and went and were trained and shown. This was a place where horses had jobs that they worked at every day. They might be your friends and they might be happy to see you, but their lives were their own, somehow. Barbie stepped onto the mounting block and got on.

Of course, Blue was perfect. Barbie was a little shaky to begin with, and Blue was careful with her, even shifting his weight to stay with her when she lost her balance a bit. An English saddle asks different things of you than a western saddle—to sit more forward, to put more weight in your heels, to use your back differently. After about ten minutes, Barbie seemed to get this, and she did make a nice trot circuit, posting rhythmically, first one direction, then the other. When the twenty minutes was over, she almost had it. I said to Jane, "She's very musical."

"That's evident," said Jane. "He's good with her, too."

I knew that.

Barbie changed her clothes and left to go to an afternoon

concert at the Mission, and Rodney took Blue, though only after I'd given him a carrot and two more lumps of sugar. Of course Mom wasn't there yet, and so I had to go into Jane's office and be told something, or a few things. Most people would have thought they were good things.

Jane said, "My heavens, girl, you have done a wonderful job with this horse! He is solid as a rock!"

"He was always a good boy."

"Yes, he was, and well disposed and responsible, but now he actually knows things, and he's very good at translating."

"What does that mean?"

"Well, your way of telling him what to do is not the same as Melinda's or Ellen's or your friend Barbie's, but he pays attention and figures it out. He's patient, but more importantly, the way they are doesn't make him nervous. You can find very nicely trained horses, but when they can't understand what the rider is getting at, they get irritated or worried, so they have a hard time being school horses. Most school horses are just dull, frankly. That's the safest type to have, and that's what most riding schools have. But he's responsive. He's quite nice."

She put her elbows on the desk and her face in her hands. The sun was shining in the window. She looked at me. She said, "I want him."

This was Dad's dream—a person he trusted asking to buy a horse that he had trained. I knew it should be my dream, too. And in a distant way, I did feel pleased with the praise.

Jane said, "You were watching Pie in the Sky. Do you wish you were riding him again? He's doing well."

I said, "I don't know what I do wish, but I don't wish that. I enjoyed him, but maybe it's because he's so good that Sophia never seems to do anything on her own, or for fun. I asked her to bring Onyx out to our place for a trail ride, but she never has time. Has she even gone down your trail to the beach?"

Jane shook her head, then said, "Sophia is very focused."

I thought that was a good word for Sophia. When she set her mind to do something, she always did it, but she always also set her mind to do something. Even at Barbie and Alexis's party, she didn't know how not to be serious.

Jane said, "What would you like to do with Blue?"

"It might be fun to take him to some shows, but he isn't going to be comfortable jumping more than three feet or 3'3", even though he'll do it." This meant, we both knew, that he would never be a star—a star jumper has to jump high, whatever his style; a star hunter has to look as though everything is easy for him and still jump four feet or 4'6"; and a star equitation horse has to go like a machine, no matter what the exercise, so that the rider can look perfect.

Jane said, "I don't know what he would have become if we'd started early with him, but he's seven or eight. What most horses can do is set by then. It's like a person being twenty-five or thirty—the years of education are behind them, and they have to make the best of what they are."

I suddenly thought of Gee Whiz jumping over the chute when the bird flew at him. I said, "What about ex-racehorses? We have one now who's eight, seventeen hands, anyway. He seems ready to do anything."

"Hmm," said Jane. "Was he good?"

"Apparently he was," I said. "He won a lot of money, raced for a long time, and remained sound."

"Well, racehorses are a little different. They often have plenty of energy and a good deal of untapped potential. They are kept fit their whole lives, so fitness is second nature to them, and they can be very intelligent—I mean, don't tell the jockeys, but it's the horse who runs the race and decides to win or not. And some sire lines have a lot of jump in them. Whether you can enlist those qualities for something new varies from horse to horse, but lots of them prefer activity to boredom. I'd like to see him."

There was a tap on the door. Jane said, "Come in!" Then she looked at me and said, "I'll give you a thousand dollars for Blue. And if I sell him to someone else for more, I'll give you ten percent of that."

The person at the door was Mom, and she was smiling. I wondered if all of this had been arranged. I said, "I'll think about it."

Jane said, "May I keep him through Monday, so that Melinda and Ellen can have another lesson on him? And your friend Barbara, too, maybe."

I said, "Okay."

I was in bed, reading. We had to read a book for English class called *A Night to Remember*, about the *Titanic*, which was a ship that they said would never sink, and then it sank first time out. The homework was due when we got back to school, in four days, and I was only to the part where the people feel a little something, but don't know that that little something is that they're hitting an iceberg. I heard the phone ring twice, and then someone must have picked it up, because it stopped ringing. A few minutes later, there was a knock at my door. I called, "Come in!" and there was Mom. She said, "Are you still awake?"

I said, "It's only eight-forty-five."

"That's true. Well, I have some bad news."

I felt myself sort of turn to stone. I was sure that the phone call had been Jane, and that something had happened to Blue. I didn't say anything.

Mom said, "I guess Sister Brooks went by to check on Brother Abner." There was a pause, then Mom hurried to say, "He was in his bed, and he had passed away."

"When was that?"

"Well, she went over there this afternoon, but when the police came, they said he had been dead since last night. They called a funeral home. We're going to have a service tomorrow, at the funeral home and the cemetery, and then another memorial service Sunday."

I said, "He seemed better Sunday. He really did. He talked and he ate most of his supper. He seemed kind of happy."

By now, Mom was sitting on the bed. She said, "Sister Brooks and I discussed that. The thing is, sometimes . . . well, do you remember a dog my parents had when you were little? Her name was Tizzy. She was half fox terrier and half something else. You liked her when you knew her."

I shook my head.

"Well, she got to be about fifteen years old, which is something like a hundred in a person, and all of a sudden, she seemed tired and sick. The thing is, she was a great guard dog—nothing moved on my parents' land without Tizzy barking about it. Well, she stopped barking—she was just too tired. Then, one day, she went outside and lay down on a hill overlooking the road to their place, and she started barking and barking. She barked for two hours, and then she went into the house and died in her bed. Your grandmother said it was like she just wanted to live the best part of her life over again, and then she was ready to go."

"He wanted one last Christmas?"

"One last good meal, one last evening with his friends, one last singing of the carols, one last celebration of our Lord. It's sadder for us, maybe, than it was for him. Your dad says that if there is anyone who is rejoicing in the presence of the Lord right now, it is Brother Abner."

"So I should be glad?"

"Well, it's hard for us to be glad when our friends go on ahead of us, because we miss them, but maybe you should be thankful that he lived a long and varied life, and that he was content with it."

We sighed.

I saw the next day that funerals are like Christmas—there are things you have to do, and in a certain order. Time moves very slowly, and there's plenty of music. Brother Abner was my only funeral. My uncle John died before I was born, and the rest of our relatives were all alive; although the brothers and the sisters seemed old to me, Brother Abner was the oldest, I found out, by ten years.

The funeral home was a big building downtown, not very

fancy from the street, but bright and clean inside. We wore nice clothes, but nothing "flashy," as Mom said. Brother Abner's casket was in the front of a paneled room with a blue carpet and no windows, much fancier than our church. There were baskets of flowers here and there. The chairs in the room were carved, and had blue tasseled cushions. There was a decorated stand in front, but when Brother Brooks and Mr. Hollingsworth and Dad stood up next to the casket to talk about Brother Abner, they didn't go behind the stand, or even look at it—they held their Bibles in their hands and spoke in regular voices. Mr. Hollingsworth even rested his hand on the casket, as if he were shaking Brother Abner's hand one last time.

I knew that sometimes Brother Abner disagreed with the others about what was right and what was wrong, but Dad chose a verse that Brother Abner would have liked: "But if any one has the world's goods and sees his brother in need, yet closes his heart against him, how does God's love abide in him? Little children, let us not love in word or in speech but in deed and in truth."

And Mr. Hollingsworth did, too: "See what love the Father has given us, that we should be called children of God; and so we are. The reason why the world does not know us is that it did not know him. Beloved, we are God's children now; it does not yet appear what we shall be, but we know that when he appears we shall be like him, for we shall see him as he is. And every one who thus hopes in him purifies himself as he is pure."

Brother Abner had once said to me, "I don't like folks

talking about who's right and who's wrong. There's too much of that. It's better to talk about the love of the Lord." Afterward, we sang two hymns, "Amazing Grace," of course, and "O God Our Help in Ages Past." Then everyone said nice things about how Brother Abner always spoke his mind, but he always had a twinkle in his eye. Most of the sisters were crying. I cried, too.

After the service, six of the brothers, including Brother Ezra Brooks, lifted up the casket and carried it out a back door I hadn't seen that led to the parking lot behind the building. They slid it into a big black hearse and closed the doors. Then we all went to our cars. Little pennants saying FUNERAL were clipped to the front windows of each car. We got into ours, and Dad waited for the others. When the hearse pulled out of the parking lot, we all went along in a line behind it. There were ten cars.

The cemetery was almost in the country—it was flat and green, surrounded by a fence, and looked out at hills to the west and fields to the east. We stood beside the grave, which had already been dug, and after we sang two more hymns, they lowered the casket, and we walked past in a line and threw flowers onto it. Then Dad and the other brothers each tossed a shovelful of dirt into the grave. There were plenty of headstones around, and it made me think of that book we'd read before the end of the semester, *Spoon River Anthology*. If Brother Abner were to wake up and speak, the way the dead people did in that book, I knew he would have some funny things to say, and I also suspected that he would not say things that he had forgotten to say, or been afraid to say, when he was alive. But I was sorry that I'd never heard more of his adventures.

Danny was at the graveside service. Maybe Mom had called him. He was wearing work clothes, and standing at the back. I saw him bow his head and move his lips in some kind of prayer. But he waved and drove off before we could talk to him. Everyone else pretended not to notice him, but I was glad he came.

Grooming Bucket

Hay Net

Chapter 10

I<small>T WAS MIDAFTERNOON BY THE TIME WE GOT HOME.</small> I <small>CHANGED</small>
into my work clothes. I can only explain what happened after
that by saying that all three of us must have been a little dazed
or tired, or something, but the fact is, someone forgot to close
the big gate. I don't know if it was me, when I got out and
opened it when we returned from the funeral. I don't know if
it was Dad, when he left in the truck to pick up something at
the Jordan Ranch. It could even have been Mom, who had
seen some wild rosemary blooming by the side of the road,
and wanted to dig it up and plant it in our garden. The thing
about us was that we never left gates open.

I was thinking about what Jane said about racehorses, so I
decided to get Gee Whiz out and clean him up. He was dusty

from nose to tail. I wasn't planning to wash him, just to curry him thoroughly, brush him, and rub him down with the chamois. He came right to the gate when I called him. I put his halter on, led him out of the pasture, and took him over to the barn, where I looped his lead rope around the bar. I could have taken him into the barn and cross-tied him, but it was sunny and pleasant outside. I started with the curry-comb. I can't say that he liked it—he was bobbing and turning his head, and then when I got to his flanks, he started lifting his back leg, not as though he was going to kick me, but as though I was tickling him. He seemed to enjoy the brushing, however, and I got to be sort of lost in it, thinking idle thoughts and humming to myself. Grooming Gee Whiz was taking a long time. But by the end of the brushing, his head was down, his right hind ankle was cocked, and he seemed to be enjoying himself. I saw that I hadn't put the chamois back in the grooming bucket, and went into the barn to find it.

There was a noise.

I turned around to see that Gee Whiz was pulling back, his head up, his ears up, and his eyes wide. The lead rope pulled off the bar, and he turned toward the house. I went after him, at first thinking only of what I thought I'd done, or should have done—he was tied, I should have put him on cross-ties, or groomed him in a stall. Then I saw him swing out around the house and head down the driveway. At first, he was trotting his big trot, and then he was galloping, and he went right out the gate. I knew Dad was gone, but as I ran past the house, I yelled for Mom. She came out onto the front porch when I was halfway to the gate, then she went back inside again.

Our driveway sloped gently to the road, which dipped as it passed us, then rose. To the left, the road continued up the hill to the Jordan Ranch. To the right, it dipped, went up slowly, then, pretty far away, made a curve. Gee Whiz went right, at first sticking to the shoulder and staying off the pavement. I guess that was a good sign. He slowed to a trot, and I could see his head turning to the left and the right. The lead rope dangled and flopped. When I got to the gate, I went out into the middle of the road and stared after him. A moment later, Mom was coming through the gate in the car. She pulled up near me and I ran around to the passenger's side and got in.

One good thing about Mom was she didn't always start out asking what had gone wrong, so you didn't feel like her first idea was to discipline you—that might come later, or she might forget about it. She said, "There he is."

Gee Whiz had paused and put his head down—probably he'd found an appetizing patch of green there that he needed to explore. Mom eased the car toward him. I rolled down my window. She said, "You have any treats?"

"I forgot them. There's a carrot in my pocket, though."

I was such an idiot.

Now Gee Whiz's head popped up and he tossed it, seeing the car just fine, and knowing exactly what it meant. He trotted forward, stepping for a moment on his rope, stopping, shaking his body to free himself, then trotting on. Mom said, "He's a smart one."

"Dad would say that's always a problem."

Mom laughed.

We eased along.

At least, he didn't race off. You never know what a horse will do in unfamiliar territory. Some horses would just panic and run, not really caring where they're going. That would be dangerous, especially if Gee Whiz ran down the slippery road and fell. But the big horse didn't seem as though he was panicking. He seemed as though he was exploring. He stayed mostly on the shoulder, only stepping into the road when the shoulder fell away or got gravelly. Sometimes he stopped and looked around, his nostrils flaring and his ears pricked. Sometimes he nosed plants, but when we got close, he trotted off. He knew we were in the car, or so it seemed. Pretty soon, we were around the curve. At that point, the road straightened and we could see about a mile ahead. Nothing coming. But after that rise, there was an intersection, and I knew that the road would get busier in both directions, and that the fenced hills of the Jordan Ranch would give way to flat fields. I did not want him running through some farmer's field. Mom got serious, too. Finally, we got sort of close to him, and she said, "You get out and I'll zoom around him and at least try to stop him from getting too far."

This was the only idea we could come up with, so I nodded. She stopped maybe ten yards from where he was looking at plants growing out of a steep hillside. I closed the door quietly, and she zipped into the left lane and went past him. Then she pulled over onto the right side of the road.

I pulled the carrot out of my pocket and held it out to Gee

Whiz. His ear flicked, but he didn't turn his head. I knew he saw it, though—a horse can see everywhere except right in front of his nose and right behind his tail. As I stepped toward him, he stepped away. He didn't run. Or trot. I stopped. He stopped. I stepped. He stepped. I took a very loud bite of the carrot and said, "Mmm. Delicious."

It was not delicious. It was kind of gunky.

But his ear flicked. By this time, I was close enough to see his lips wrinkle. Maybe he was imagining eating the carrot.

The thing was, he was a beautiful horse, strong and majestic—way more self-confident-looking than Pie in the Sky, or even Onyx. It was like he always knew that crowds had looked at him, crowds had cheered him. Something about his face said that having done many things and been many places, he could do anything he put his mind to. I murmured, "Gee Whiz. Gee Whiz. It's much nicer at home than it is out here. We have such nice hay and some very good oats, and apples and more carrots."

His ears flicked again.

I stepped toward him, and he trotted off.

Now I spun right around, just like a dancer, and I trotted off myself, up the road away from him. But the sun was in the west, and if I looked down and a little to the left, I could see his shadow. He was behind me, coming with me, not going away. I pretended not to know and not to care. I slowed down and paused. I heard his steel shoes on the pavement, *clop clop, clop clop*. I put the carrot back in my pocket, and pretended to be strolling along, looking at plants—rosemary, yes; French broom, yes; Indian paintbrush, yes; ceanothus, yes. How interesting. And the sky! Very blue! And the side of the hill! Brown and dusty! And the wire fencing! Were those cows up there?

He nudged my hip with his nose, but I walked away. When he came up and nudged me again, I pulled out the carrot and let him have it without looking at him, but then when he was eating it, I turned and said, "Oh, what a nice horse. Such a beauty to find walking down the road." I reached for his lead rope and then started petting him. He snorted, but not out of nervousness, just as if to say, "Okay, you got me." I started walking down the road.

Mom pulled up beside us. She said, "My heaven. That was scary."

I petted Gee Whiz on the cheek. "Only to us, I think."

While we were stopped there, Dad came up behind Mom's car in the truck, slowed, stared, and then waved and went around us. Mom said, "Oh dear."

It was then that I knew that she had planned to keep this little adventure a secret.

I said, "Okay, well, since we're out here, Gee Whiz and I are going to go for a little walk."

"You sure he'll be okay?"

"I don't think he wants to run away. I think he wants to investigate."

"If you say so."

We came to our gate. Dad had left it open. Mom drove through, and I closed it after her. Then Gee Whiz and I headed up the road toward the entrance to the Jordan Ranch, just to see what we could see.

Sometimes they say that a horse has "presence." I never quite knew what they meant by this. Every horse is more or less large. Even a pony like Gallant Man weighs about six hundred pounds. A full-sized horse weighs a thousand pounds or more. My yearling, Jack (soon a two-year-old, according to the Jockey Club), never let you forget that he was around—either he was looking at you or nuzzling you or asking to play or showing off. Blue was beautiful and quiet. His presence made me feel good. But Gee Whiz had something more, some electricity, some intensity that the others didn't have. He walked along nicely—not pushing ahead or giving me trouble in any way. I didn't even have to hurry to keep up with him. I remembered an expression we had talked about in history class—it was noblesse oblige. It meant that a nobleman was being kind and courteous because it was part of his job to do that. Could a horse feel that? It felt like it as we walked along, Gee Whiz not following me or pulling me, but accompanying me, looking here and there, pausing from time to time. We went about half a mile down the road, to where we could see the gate to the Jordan Ranch, and turned back. By the time we got home, the sun was pretty low in the sky. I undid the gate and pushed it open. Gee Whiz stood quietly while I closed it and bolted it. I said, "Look the other way. This one doesn't work that well, either."

Dad was in the barn, piling hay in the wheelbarrow. I said hi and walked past, to the gate of the gelding pasture. I opened it. I have to say, Gee Whiz paused before he walked in, but he did walk in. Oh My gave him a brilliant whinny. I could tell Mom had told Dad all about the escape, because he didn't say anything to me. That would be for later. All he said was, "Did you like the service?"

I nodded.

"I think Brother Abner would have liked it."

"I'm glad we had a nice day."

"We need rain, but yes, I am, too."

Danny called that night. Mom answered and asked him to come for supper the next night. Then she said the words "prime rib." We didn't often have prime rib, but I guess Dad had gotten a present from Mr. Jordan. When she got off the phone, she said, "Jerry's coming, too. He wants to see Beebop."

I said, "If you'd asked me a few weeks ago which horse was going to be the troublemaker, I would have said Beebop."

Dad laughed. "Beebop is just a working man with a special talent."

The next day, Danny came early and took Marcus for a ride, to see how he was coming along. I was tacking up Oh My, so we went over to the arena together. Marcus was like the kid at school who does everything right and is always wearing nice clothes, and no one pays attention to him, even so. You sort of had to remember to say, "He is nice, isn't he?" and even while you were saying that, you were thinking about someone more glamorous, like Gee Whiz, whom we could see staring at us from the pasture while we rode.

Maybe that's why I talked all the time we were walking out, and didn't notice Danny's face getting stiffer and stiffer, like Dad's, of course, when he is thinking that a child's being seen and not heard is a good thing. First, I talked about Jack, and how beautiful he was. I had been thinking about him all week and, I mean, Gee Whiz made him look like a baby still, but he was getting bigger and more graceful, and seemed older. I wondered how long horses trained before they went to the track, and then in their first race.

"No idea," said Danny.

Still, that was exciting. Of course, that raised another issue, about whether we would ever get to see him run.

"Don't count on it," said Danny.

That shut me up about racing, so I started in about Jerry. What time was he coming? Maybe he would bring something good from San Francisco. Barbie had thought he was lots of fun. We should do something with Beebop, at least let him run around in the arena. He seemed not to have much personality, way less than Gee Whiz.

Which, of course, got me back thinking about racing. Gee Whiz, I said, made you think that the whole world was very interesting and exciting, and even though he'd only gotten half a mile down the road, he *wanted* to go. He had been more places than I had, maybe more places than Dad or Mom had—France, for heaven's sake! Kentucky! Arkansas, Los Angeles, San Francisco, Saratoga.

Danny said, "I wouldn't take a free ticket to Arkansas."

And soon it would be a new year! What was Danny doing New Year's Eve? Going out with Leah, I guessed. Well, that was more fun than sitting around reading *A Night to Remember* and listening to Simon and Garfunkel for the millionth time. I couldn't wait until something would finally happen—

"Yes, you can," said Danny. "You can wait. And just so you know, Leah and I broke up, for good."

"Before New Year's Eve?"

"Best time," said Danny.

Now we rode in silence. The horses walked along, *clop clop*, and yes, Marcus was quite calm and good for such an inexperienced horse. Finally, I said, "Why is that?"

"Because I am not going to bring in the new year making promises that I can't keep."

"It was your idea?"

Another silence, then, "Yes."

Now we were quiet. We finished our ride and went back to the barn, where Danny turned on the dusty old radio, very low. The song was one I liked, but it was creepy—"Paint It, Black," by the Rolling Stones. I had heard it lots of times before, but now it made me think of Brother Abner's funeral—"I see a line of cars, and they're all painted black." Danny turned it up, and I had to walk out of the barn because I had gone from being excited to being really sad. I stood there, waiting until I was really sure that I wasn't going to cry.

When Jerry showed up a little later, Danny was still quiet, but Jerry didn't seem to notice. He talked and chatted, and not only to Beebop. Beebop was clearly glad to see Jerry. He trotted over to the fence, and when Lincoln came with him, he lifted his hind foot—"This guy is mine!" Jerry had a cut-up apple, which he gave to Beebop piece by piece. I told him about the big escape, when all the geldings got out and a few of the mares, and how we found Beebop in the front yard, minding his own business and grazing. Jerry laughed, and said, "He's a food horse, all right."

"What does that mean?"

"Oh, one of the hands who had horses where he used to be said there's food horses and there's play horses. With a play horse, the rider shows up at the same time as the hay, and the play horse takes a bite of his hay, then comes to the gate and wants to know what's up. A food horse only has eyes for the hay, no matter what's up."

I decided that Jack was a play horse.

I helped him brush Beebop down. His coat was thick, and he had very long whiskers as well as feathery pasterns, so he took a lot of grooming, but Jerry wasn't in a hurry. While he brushed him, he petted him, and tickled him around the eyes. When he did this, Beebop sort of seemed to doze. I watched Jerry. He really liked his horse and saw beauty in him that I certainly did not. At one point, he did something I'd never seen a guy do—he kissed him on the nose.

We led Beebop to the big arena. The horse walked along, lagging a little behind, blowing out air, one time stopping to rub his nose on his knee. He looked like a trail horse over at the stables, ready to walk the trail to the ocean and back for the thousandth time. And even when we took his halter off and put him in the arena, he at first didn't do much—like the others, he walked around and checked out what was in there. He looked up the hill. He watched Rusty chasing something, without reacting. He took a deep sigh. Then he started trotting. He didn't have a big or a pretty trot. It was just a trot. He trotted here and there, slowed to the walk, picked up the trot again. Finally, he found the spot—a little damp, a little deep and sandy, just right. He dropped to his knees and flopped over, then he rolled and rolled, more like a dog than a horse, with his legs in the air. He did not have prominent withers, so maybe that's why he was good at going all the way over—not many horses go back and forth, but Beebop did. Then he sort of lifted himself onto his right haunch and did something I had never seen a horse do, which was almost sitting like a dog and scratching his hip against the sand—he looked for a moment like he was having a hard time getting to his feet. Jerry said, "The first time I saw that, I thought something was wrong with him, but he just likes to get everything as gritty as possible."

Beebop stood up, shook himself off, and was still for a moment. Then he leapt into the air and took off bucking and kicking down the long side of the arena, his head low, his ears pinned, and his body almost vertical to the ground. At buck number two, he started squealing. He bucked and squealed eight times, each more violent than the last, and then galloped for ten or twenty strides, but he wasn't a Thoroughbred—there was no fun in galloping for him. He went back to the trot, this time with slightly bigger strides than before, and trotted here and there. Finally, he came over to Jerry and received another piece of apple. By now, he was quiet as you please. His ears were relaxed, and he was perfectly friendly.

I said, "He likes that."

"He does."

"Does he, say, go up to the cowboy he's just bucked off and ask him for a lump of sugar?"

"That would be funny. But no. At the rodeo, he's in a different mood. He knows it's a competition and he's got to be serious. The bronc rider is his rival. He wants to beat him."

"He doesn't want to kill him?"

"I never get that feeling. Anyway, it would be hard to run rodeos with rogue horses. They've got to cooperate when they're not in the ring. It's not like a bullfight, a fight to the death. It's a game. You ask me, both the horse and the rider know it's a game, but they've got to play it wholehearted, or they don't get a good score. And the horse has to get a good score, because if it looks too easy, the rider's score suffers." Beebop walked away and came back again. Jerry smoothed some of the sand off his neck and said, "Beebop's tough but fair—he gives it all he's got, he bucks high, and he's got a few moves that are a little unexpected, but . . . I don't know. He's got a rhythm, so they tell me he's fun to ride."

I couldn't imagine this.

I said, "He doesn't kick the other horses. I guess, looking at him, I'd think he'd use that against them."

"Never has," said Jerry. "But I keep him unshod behind if he's turned out. You never know if they're going to take a dislike to someone." He put the halter on Beebop and took him through the gate. I headed back to the house while they walked along the outside of the fence, looking for tufts of grass.

Jerry had brought something to go with the prime rib, two artichokes that he'd picked up on the way down and a stem of something. When I went in the house, Mom was pulling the things off the stem, and I saw that they were Brussels sprouts. I made a face. But when Jerry came in the house, he cooked both the Brussels sprouts and the artichokes, and I had to admit that they were good—I would have thought that you could not do a thing with a Brussels sprout that would take away the bitter flavor, but he steamed them, cut them in half, poured some of the olive oil he brought over them, and stuck them in the oven until they were brown. The artichokes he served like Mrs. Goldman had, boiled and sitting up in bowls. His sauce looked like mayonnaise, except that it was actually lemony and good. Mom's prime rib was, of course, delicious, so this supper ended up being maybe the best meal of the year.

While we were eating, Jerry asked about the other horses, and Dad said everyone was fine, but he and Danny both looked a little mad, so I suspected that while Jerry and I had been outside, Danny and Dad had been having it out about Gee Whiz. Of course, Dad would have said that enough is enough, the horse had to go once the payment had run out, and maybe Danny would have said that the horse belonged to him now, and then Dad would have said that that was a stupid thing to do, take on a horse when your life is about to change, and after that, I had no idea what they would have said. But if I'd been there, I would have spoken up, "I'll take him." No one asked me, though. We all knew that by this time next week, Danny would have had his physical, so maybe it was best to put off all disagreements until then.

But after all, it was me who was called into the living room and told to sit down because we had to have a serious conversation. It was New Year's Eve. The pie that Mom had made for the service the next day was in the oven—I could smell it.

When I sat down on the sofa, Dad and Mom looked more concerned than angry, and why would they be angry? I mean, except for me not telling about how Gee Whiz got out that first time. And even if that was my fault, I didn't think it was a sitting-on-the-couch-for-a-serious-discussion sort of thing.

Dad cleared his throat.

Then he said, "I have asked the Lord whether this is my business, Abby. And your mom and I have also talked about it." He glanced at her. "However, it was purely by accident that we know this, so I haven't said anything, hoping that you would come to me for my advice."

Now I really didn't know what they were talking about.

He coughed.

"Anyway, when Dan was here yesterday before supper, I asked him point-blank about what happens when a colt goes to the racetrack, and I got some information out of him that I find a little startling, but horse racing is always said to be a rich man's sport, and I guess there's a reason for that. Well, anyway, he told me that when a horse is at the racetrack, the trainer charges twenty"—now he started coughing, as if he couldn't actually get the word out—"dollars per day, that's six hundred dollars a month, which is eight times what we charge." Then he said, "I don't know what they pay for with all of that money. The hay must be dipped in gold, but even the cheapest trainer up north in the Bay Area gets fifteen."

Mom's head was moving back and forth—not as though she was shaking her head no, more as though she was stunned by the figures. I might have been stunned by the figures myself, but I really didn't understand them. Six hundred dollars every month! Or anyway, four hundred and fifty. We were the kind of people who hesitated before buying a dress for forty dollars, or riding boots for sixty—and the riding boots were supposed to last you the next twenty years. I did have a hundred dollars in my bank account—well, ninety-four, because of Christmas, but that was not quite five days at the racetrack.

I said, "Even if Mr. Matthews splits it with us, that's ten dollars a day." Nine days.

Dad said, "When they get to the track as two-year-olds, according to Roscoe Pelham, it takes a while for them to settle in and get fit enough for a race. Sometimes four or five months, and according to him, the longer the better, because you want the fitness to come on slow and settle in. They're more likely to break down if you push them too hard."

"So," said Mom, in a sort of strangled voice, "that could be, like, twenty-four hundred or even three thousand dollars before a horse races, and then, when he does, he probab— might not win."

I said, "Jane offered me a thousand dollars for Blue."

Mom and Dad exchanged a glance.

Dad said, "I know that. Your mom overheard that. But even so, supporting a racehorse might not be the best place to put that money. *If* you sell the horse. But he's a good horse. . . ."

"You always say it's never too soon to sell a horse."

"I do say that, but that's partly a joke and partly a good-luck charm. Every day that you have a horse, something could go wrong. We all know that, but we also know that there are better times in a horse's life to sell him, and better times in

198

the year to sell him, too. And what we always hope for is that the right owner will come along. We wait for that if we can afford to."

"What if Mr. Matthews says he'll pay for it, like he did this training?"

"I don't see how we can accept that kind of an offer, Abby."

They both sighed.

Then Dad said, "Having Jack at Vista del Canada is a piece of good luck—Mr. Matthews and the man who owns that place did a little bartering, and it worked out. Since we had already seen to Jack's expenses for twenty-one months, we could look at it as a fair deal all around. But this is different. Jack would go to a trainer who would have to be paid every month. Mr. Matthews uses several different trainers, I guess, because he has horses at different tracks, and mostly in the East." He was quiet for a long moment, then looked at me the way parents do when they really want you to pay attention. His voice sort of deepened. "When horses go into the world, the world always turns out to be a big, big place."

Well, Gee Whiz was the perfect example of that, wasn't he?

I said, "What do you want me to do?"

Mom said, "We don't want you to do anything. We just want you to know how things work. We don't want anything to come as a big surprise down the road."

"You don't want me to get my hopes up."

"Well. No. We don't," said Dad.

"Did Danny tell you my hopes were up?"

Finally, Dad said, "Danny and I didn't talk about you. He

told me that the horse looks good, that they like him, and what he found out about how it works. That's all."

But were my hopes up? And what for? I had no idea. I went up to my room and stared out the window at the gelding pasture, wishing that Jack were back in there, back to being a playful, cute colt, Jack the Pest, always curious and funny, and that there were no choices to be made.

Bridle Without Reins

Snaffle Bit with Reins

Chapter 11

Maybe Mom and Dad felt bad about this serious conversation, because when Barbie called a little later and asked
me over for supper (she knew I couldn't spend the night on a
Saturday night), they said yes without even saying "Well, I
don't know" first. Mom agreed to drive me over, and Barbie
said that her mom would drive me home.

I would not say it was a party, but Leslie was there, too,
which was interesting enough to make me forget for the time
being that I had no idea what was going to happen with Jack.
When I got there, the twins and Leslie were out on the deck,
talking about what they'd done that day—they'd taken Leslie's dog to the beach. Leslie had a hunting dog, a pointer,
who loved the beach. The three of them were walking along

way at the far end, and the dog was jumping in and out of the waves as if they were warm rather than freezing cold. Leslie and Alexis were chatting about hikes up into the mountains, and Barbie was lagging behind them, picking up pieces of clamshell, when the dog pointed for about a second, at a seagull, and then began to approach it, moving so slowly and carefully that Leslie didn't realize what he was doing. And the seagull didn't, either. "I was just wondering what Bingo was thinking."

I said, "What was he thinking?"

"At that very moment, he ran and grabbed the seagull as it was taking off. He never did that before."

"Rusty killed a bobcat. It was a little tiny bobcat, but it was a bobcat."

Alexis said, "I thought Rusty's job was to save baby animals."

Then we told Leslie about Staccato, who, right on cue, stalked across the deck with his tail in the air, just twitching the very tip. When he got exactly to the middle of the four of us, he sat down and started grooming his whiskers, as if to say, "Oh, you're here—admire me!" We laughed.

Barbie said, "We did sneak back down the beach with our faces averted, as if we didn't know who this dog was."

Leslie said, "My dad got him for free from a guy who told us he wasn't a gun dog. So, you never know."

Mrs. Goldman came to the door and said, "Dinner's almost ready. You'd better have the exposition pretty soon."

Both Barbie and Alexis grinned.

Barbie said, "You two have to be fitted with blindfolds."

Leslie laughed, and said, "I'll bet!"

Well, we were allowed to climb the stairs on our own, but when we came to Barbie and Alexis's bathroom door, Alexis said, "Okay, put your hands over your eyes."

I realized that the paintings were finished. I closed my eyes and put my hands over them, then someone took my elbow and I heard the sound of the door opening. I did not open my eyes. Whoever was holding my elbow moved me a little bit here and there, then turned me and halted me. Then I felt something against my back, which I realized was Leslie. Finally, Alexis said, "Stop, look, and listen!" which made me laugh, because that's what our kindergarten teacher always said, one finger pointed in the air. I opened my eyes. Right in front of me was Barbie's solstice painting, deep red, flat, the horizon sunlit from the edge, fading above to stars and darkness. When I'd looked for a while at this, Barbie turned Leslie and me to the right, which was west. Now I was looking at Alexis's ocean painting, the fog pale and vapory, and the tops of the rocks dark and wet-looking. The horizon was bright and blue, as if the fog was coming onto the land, but the ocean was sunny behind it. We were now turned to the north, and there was Alexis's field of lupines, just a long green slope to a distant road, and beyond that a dark hillside. But the lupines, purple and green and painted one by one, spilled down the slope so luxuriantly that you could almost smell them. Now we turned again, and there was Barbie's second painting, and it was very strange. She had taken the view from the living room—the very view we had been looking at when we were talking about Leslie's dog and watching Staccato—and she'd reduced it and reproduced it on the bathroom wall, including on the door, which was closed. Even the time of day was the same—toward dusk, with long shadows reaching into the canyon. Down in the left-hand corner, small but beautifully done, was Blue, staring off into the distance, his mouth slightly open, as if he was whinnying. I said, "Wow!"

Leslie said, "These are great." She put her hand out and just touched the solstice painting with the tip of her finger.

Barbie glanced at me, and said, "I wanted to paint him galloping, but that's a lot harder, so I just painted him calling me," and she laughed. "Alexis completely hogged the purple and I was lucky to get any green at all."

"Well, you used up all the red."

Now they were both giggling.

Alexis said, "You're the first to see them besides Mom. We haven't even let Dad in. He comes in tonight."

I looked up. They'd even done the ceiling, in shades of blue, with the stars getting bigger and more numerous to the east. No moon. The bathroom, which was fairly small, felt huge.

Alexis said, "Mom says when we come home in the spring, we can try doing something to the sink and the bathtub. Enamel paint might work. There are also these acrylic paints that dry to be waterproof."

Leslie said, "Does your mom let you do anything you want?"

Barbie said, "She always says 'within reason,' which means we have to come up with a reason that she actually believes."

I took this to mean yes.

For supper, we had quiche made with ham and mush-rooms, along with spinach as a salad and homemade French bread—apparently, when Marie was there, she had taught Mrs. Goldman how to make long baguettes, and so every menu had to start with bread and end with something else French. This time it ended with crème brûlée, which was a vanilla custard sort of thing with a burnt-sugar crust over the top, and so delicious that Leslie took three bites. What was funny was that Barbie and Alexis spoke to their mother only in French, even though she spoke to them in English. Every so often, after she said something to them, they turned to one another and carried on a very fast conversation with many gestures and nods of the head. Finally, Mrs. Goldman said, "You girls are trying to make me crazy, but it isn't going to work. Abby? Leslie? Would you like anything else? A cup of tea, maybe? Mint tea?"

Alexis said, "Here's the problem with California."

Leslie laughed, and Barbie said, "Do tell."

"New Year's Eve comes here almost last. The only worse place is Hawaii. I mean, in Australia and New Zealand, and then Rome and London, it's all over, and in New York, they'll start celebrating at Times Square in about an hour and a half. By the time we get to do it, everyone else in the world is tired of the whole thing."

"Where would you do it?" said Leslie.

Alexis said, "Australia, for sure. It's summer! Fireworks and a swim!"

Mrs. Goldman of course said Paris. She had been there for New Year's right after the war—it wasn't a huge celebration, but it was full of relief, and hopeful. Mr. Goldman had spent his high school years sneaking away from his parents' house in Trenton and getting as close as he could to Times Square—he made it once, his junior year. Barbie said London, and Leslie said the North Pole, but she didn't know why. I couldn't think of a place, so I didn't say anything.

Barbie came along when Mrs. Goldman drove me home. As soon as we were out of their neighborhood, she said, "Are we sure that this is the same Leslie we've known since kindergarten? Maybe what that camp that she went to does is substitute entirely different people for the ones who show up on day one."

"At school, we just do what she says. Sophia does what she says. Lucia does what she says. I do what she says. Even Kyle Gonzalez does what she says."

"No!" said Barbie.

"Yes. We had to do the dissection of the fetal pig, and she told him how to hold the scalpel, and he held it the way she said. I saw from across the room. She talked, he cut, and she wrote down the notes."

"We haven't gotten to dissecting yet," said Barbie.

"It was pretty bad. Stella said the smell was making her want to puke, so she brought her father's bottle of Brut cologne and poured it into the pig when the teacher wasn't looking. Then it really stank!"

"In the Middle Ages, artists bought corpses from grave robbers and dissected them to see how the body worked. You have to see all the layers."

We drove in silence, then she said, "I guess she's going to

another camp this summer. She's already sent in her application. It's in Canada. They canoe from lake to lake for six weeks, portaging between lakes. They gather herbs and fish for their own food."

I hadn't heard this. I said, "I get the feeling she'll do anything."

Barbie said, "I'd like to be that way."

Her mom said, "I thought you were that way already."

They dropped me off, and we spent a quiet New Year's Eve like we always did, Mom and Dad yawning at about nine-thirty, me offering to do the last check on the horses. The question still lingered in my mind—where would I spend New Year's if I had the chance? Danny was surely at a party, Leslie was still at the Goldmans', Jerry was probably cooking something somewhere. The only thing I could think of was something I couldn't do, that no one did—it was riding my horse across a field lit by the full moon, no danger anywhere, no holes or cliffs or wild animals, just a long, smooth gallop, me leaning forward in my two-point position, hearing his breathing, feeling his warmth, sensing his strides as they opened and closed, my hands light on the reins, his mouth light in my hands. The old year would disappear into the new one easy as you please, marked only by a jump in a fence line, up and over and onward.

Miss Cumberland had taken attendance and already started telling us that we had to start moving toward the modern era, and so jump to the year 1066 and go on from there. Kyle Gonzalez, without even raising his hand, said, "William the

Conqueror." Miss Cumberland nodded but put her finger to her lips. Just then Sophia opened the door, looked around for me, walked over, plopped her books on the desk, and sat down. Miss Cumberland said, "Do you have an excuse, Sophia?"

Sophia said, "I had to go to the bathroom."

Everyone laughed.

Miss Cumberland said, "I mean a written excuse, of course."

Sophia shook her head.

Miss Cumberland cleared her throat and continued while Sophia started staring at me. Finally, when she knew I was looking at her, she turned up her right hand, which was on the table. On her palm, she had written, "May I come for a trail ride Saturday?"

She knew I would want to giggle, but I didn't dare. I just nodded. We opened our books, and Miss Cumberland explained about the Saxons and the Angles and the Vikings and Normandy, which was in France. All the time the Romans were busy in Rome, other tribes were spreading across Europe from the southeast to the northwest, bringing their languages with them. She reached up and pulled down a map. Sophia lifted her other hand. Written on the palm of that one was "9 a.m.?"

I nodded, but this time I did laugh, and this time Miss Cumberland did say, "Is something funny, Abigail?"

I apologized.

When class was finished, Sophia stood up and, as usual, marched out of the room without saying anything. But I noticed that her hair was down, swaying back and forth as she marched.

That afternoon, Dad was outside the high school in his truck, pulling the trailer. We were off to pick up Blue. And it was finally raining, which meant that I had to run across the parking lot and throw myself into the truck, but also that Dad was humming a little and in a very good mood. The high school was much closer to the stables than to our house, but even in that short distance, the rain intensified and intensified, until Dad had to slow down because the wipers weren't doing a good enough job of clearing the windshield. He even had to turn off the radio, because the sound of the rain on the roof of the truck was so steady and loud.

When we got to the stables, Jane was out in her rubber boots and her English raincoat that went all the way down past her knees. When Dad started backing up, she waved us almost into the stable yard. Every ring was deserted, every tree was dripping, every jump was glistening with moisture, every horse was huddled into his stall, wrapped in a blanket of some kind, eating his hay. As we led Blue out into the downpour, fifteen heads popped over stall doors, ears forward, mouths chewing, seeming to say, "Oh, you poor poor thing!"

Blue was good, though. He loaded right up and stood quietly all the way home. As we drove east, the downpour dissipated, until it was just a drizzle at our house, but Dad was hopeful—we had just beaten it, that was all. It would follow us and green up the hillsides.

And it did. That night, the horses gathered under the trees while the rain drummed on the roof, pounded the windows, replenished the water tanks, made puddles everywhere. When Dad came in after the morning feeding, while I was eating my oatmeal, he said, "Four inches in the gauge." He was grinning.

It was sunny by noon, and bright by the time I was heading home on the school bus. I couldn't ride Blue because the arena was wet, so I cleaned my tack and swept the barn aisle and even went upstairs and straightened the shelves in my room. Then I started my homework, an "imaginative paper" about what I would have done if I had been on the *Titanic* the night it went down. I knew what Mom and Dad would have done—they would have prayed. So I wrote that down. Dad would have opened his Bible and found a passage for guidance, so I did that. The passage I found was one that Dad had marked (which was probably why I found it). It was from the book of Job. It read, "The Lord gave, and the Lord has taken away; blessed be the name of the Lord." Normally, the book of Job kind of scared me, but I thought this was a pretty good passage for my paper about the *Titanic*.

The next day, we all knew, was the day of Danny's physical. When I got home, Mom was pacing around the kitchen, and Rusty was staring at her through the back window—Rusty knew how to be worried. Mom kissed my cheek in sort of a distracted way, and put a snack on the table, two graham crackers and a banana, but she didn't say anything—she just went into the living room and checked whether the phone was working, then replaced it very carefully on the hook. I went up to my room to change, then out the front door to the barn. I didn't know what to hope for. Mom did not want Danny to go into the army. Dad didn't say what he wanted, but I knew that he thought that if your country needed you, the right sort of man went and did what was asked of him. I also knew that he was sure that Danny was strong and smart. There were guys who thrived in the army because they had their wits about them. I only wanted what Danny wanted, but I wondered if he knew, deep down, what it was that he wanted.

Blue came to the gate as soon as he saw me. His coat had dried with that clean roughness that horses get in a good rain, so all I had to do was brush him with the soft brush and tack him up. The arena was good already—the rain had soaked down into the dry footing and given it a little bounce. I mounted from the mounting block. While I was tightening my girth, Gee Whiz gave a loud whinny, long and plaintive, and Oh My answered him. Blue paid no attention.

We walked to the arena. When we got there, I opened the gate from on his back (something he had never done before he came), then I closed it again (ditto). I asked him for an easy walk on a long rein—very good. I asked him for some loopy turns, a big figure eight, a small figure eight, some rein-backs, some transitions into and out of the walk, the trot, the canter. His transition from the halt to the canter was a great pleasure. I asked him again. He did it again. When he was well warmed up, we cantered in a leisurely way around the arena, crossed through the middle, did a flying change. I asked him to speed up. He did the best he could, but when I was no longer asking him, he slowed down again, to his gentle, not very exciting lope. Best not to be exciting. For Blue, exciting meant nervous.

Once I was finished with him, I got Oh My out and tacked

her up. Then I put Nobby on the lead rope, and I took the two of them out the gate and up and down the road, since the trail and the hills were very wet. All we did was walk, and three cars passed, but they behaved themselves. We went way past the gate to the Jordan Ranch. It was green all the way. I figured that the next day I would ride Nobby and lead Oh My, and they could both learn the same lesson.

It got dark while I was giving the horses their hay. I went inside. Dad was doing some bills while Mom finished setting the table. I washed up. No one said anything. Just by looking at the telephone, I could see that it had been silent as a rock. We had hash made from the leftovers of the prime rib—one of my favorite things, the meat all savory and ground up with the potatoes and onions. There was plenty of it, too, and maybe because we had nothing to say, we all ate a lot—cleaned our plates, cleaned the serving bowl, ate the last green bean. The phone was a dead thing.

I helped Mom with the dishes, hung around for a few minutes, then gave up and went to my room. Of course right then the phone rang. It rang seven times. I guess after all the waiting, no one dared to pick it up.

But then I heard Dad say, "Oh, hi! Nice to hear from you."

He would not say that to Danny. Too formal.

And then, "Abby!"

It was Jane, not Danny. She said, "What a rain! Did you feel horrible making poor Blue stay out in that downpour? With the water just running down his cheeks and into his eyes and turning the footing to mud?"

I said, "Sort of."

She said, "Oh, darling! Well, you shouldn't. It doesn't matter what the weather is in California, it's a paradise compared to everywhere else in the world. I'm sure he thought it was invigorating."

I said, "I hope so."

"But I have to soften you up. I really want that horse. It was so teeming yesterday that I didn't tell you how good he was with both Melinda and Ellen. You know, the second time is the one that matters, and he was just as kind as could be, but willing. And Melinda feels comfortable on him—for certain she's going to grow another couple of inches, and she's quite long in the leg as it is. Of course, Ellen is about as big as a button up there on his back, but she thinks it's thrilling." She paused. "I also taught another student. Do you remember little Robert? He was in the show. I believe he cried. But he did fine on Blue, who is six times as agreeable as his horrible ancient pony who is a zillion years old and learned back in the nineteenth century to never listen to a mere child." Another pause. I felt sort of overwhelmed. And Dad kept looking at me. Jane said, "I am raising my offer to twelve hundred, and you know that you can ride him out here, and take lessons, and show him, too. You don't have to own a horse to enjoy him, Abby—in fact, many experienced equestrians would say that not owning a horse is the ideal situation."

"My dad would say that."

"Well, think about it."

I said that I would.

Danny never called.

And he didn't call the next day, either.

I heard Mom and Dad have a little discussion about whether Danny was stubborn, afraid, or "independent." It reminded me of the bad old days after Danny and Dad had their big fight, and we hardly saw Danny at all.

But Friday afternoon, I got off the school bus at the very moment that Danny was turning into our driveway in his truck. I hugged my books to my chest and went to open the gate for him. He drove straight past the house to the barn, and I ran after him. When he got out of the truck, he said, "Go get your work clothes on. We have something to do."

I knew it was about Gee Whiz.

Mom's car was outside, but she wasn't in the house, so I decided she and Dad had gone somewhere, which maybe was good, since maybe Danny wanted to do a few things on his own. I pulled on my jeans and a jacket, then ran out the back door, only stopping to put on my boots.

He was already brushing Gee Whiz. I grabbed a brush and helped him. The horse was so tall that I could only see Danny's feet underneath and the brim of his hat on the other side. Gee Whiz seemed to enjoy the attention—he stood more quietly than he had the previous time. Even so, I wasn't going to leave him alone to pull back—once they've tried it and succeeded, they often try it again. Danny seemed in a good mood. We didn't know the results of his physical, but maybe he did. However, he wasn't saying anything about it to me, and I was afraid to ask. When he got to smoothing a rag over Gee Whiz's face to clean off some of the dust, he finally broke the silence. "Jem Jarrow came over to the Marble Ranch this morning when I was working a couple of the calves with Happy, and I asked him something."

"What?"

"How to start retraining an ex-racehorse."

"What are you going to retrain him to do?" I had never seen a cow horse nearly as big as Gee Whiz.

"You told me yourself that he jumped 3'3"—or three feet, anyway—without even thinking about it."

I thought, "Uh-oh," but I said, "So what did Jem say?"

"Well, you do him the usual way—you teach him to step under and use his back feet, because at the racetrack, the back end is there for pushing off, but he said, 'Sometimes those racehorses don't know that it can actually do anything.'"

"What does that mean?"

"They get into habits—they always race to the left, for example, so how they use their haunches is always cocked a little so that they can get more power to the left. Or they dig in with the front end, which shifts their weight forward. Look at this." He pointed to Gee Whiz's neck. The muscles along the lower part bulged slightly more than the muscles along the crest. "That's from pulling rather than pushing. They get in the habit of using their bodies in a certain way, and you have to recognize that it's a habit rather than a fault."

He led him over to the pen and took him through the gate, picking up the flag that was leaning against the fence post. I closed the gate.

Gee Whiz looked too big for the pen, just the way he had the time Barbie and I had put him in there, but as before, once Danny waved the flag, and he backed away, turned, and started trotting, it was clear that he was perfectly comfortable. This time, he shortened his strides by lifting his back and bending; he didn't look at all awkward. Danny let him go around three times, then stepped slightly in front of him and lifted the flag again. Gee Whiz gave him a quizzical look, then paused, and trotted off the other way. I said, "Right answer."

Danny grinned.

I said, "We did this before. It looks like he learned something."

Gee Whiz didn't buck or kick out. He just kept making smooth turns and going the other way. Danny let him do this until he came down to a walk on his own, and then Danny stepped back, and Gee Whiz approached him. Danny slipped the training halter with the long lead rope over his head and tied it.

The first time Danny asked Gee Whiz to step over in the Jem Jarrow way, the horse gave him the look again, that "What in the world are you talking about?" look that I'd never seen on the face of any other horse. I thought of what Jane had said, about a horse "translating" what the rider or trainer is asking for, and I decided that was his look—not scared, not resentful, not indifferent, but curious. Danny went up to him, bent his neck around, lifted his nose, nudged him on the haunch with his hand. Gee Whiz seemed to say, "Oh, I understand! Sure!" He stepped over.

He stepped over several times to the right, then several times to the left. Then Danny did one of my favorite things— he slipped the rope over Gee Whiz's head and ran it along his side until it came around his haunches, then he applied a little pressure. Gee Whiz stood there, big and white, looking off into the distance. Danny applied more pressure. Gee Whiz stiffened his head and neck, which is something horses do when they feel pressure. Danny pulled a little harder. Gee Whiz lowered his head, and the rope along his side dropped so that I could see it along his legs. There was a pause, but then he turned his head toward the pressure, and a moment later, he swiveled his body. Once he was facing Danny, Danny petted him, and said, "Smarty-pants."

We called this move the corkscrew. They did the corkscrew several times, until finally Gee Whiz wasn't giving Danny the opportunity to apply pressure at all—as soon as he felt the rope across his tail, he turned.

Danny was now in an even better mood, as good as I'd seen in a couple of weeks. He stepped up beside Gee Whiz's neck, on the left side, facing backward. He gently put his hand on the far side of Gee Whiz's nose. They stood there for a moment, then Gee Whiz bent his neck and brought his head around. Danny held it until Gee Whiz relaxed. When Danny took his hand away, Gee Whiz kept his neck curled for about a second, then straightened it. Danny did this on both sides, too. The point was to always remind him that he wasn't a plank. He was a supple, athletic animal—the more supple, the more athletic. Danny said, "I didn't think he would be so cooperative. I thought he would be a lot stiffer."

"He doesn't move in the pasture like he's stiff. He moves in the pasture like he can do anything he wants to."

"Let's go over to the arena."

I said, "What else did Jem Jarrow say? This is the same stuff we would use with any horse."

"He said, 'Always let him go forward.'"

"What does that mean?"

"I guess it means that at least for the first while, if we lift the rein from the saddle and ask him to come under, it's just a little. He thinks they're so used to going forward that they get nervous if you slow them down too much."

I thought of the trot and the canter and the gallop I had seen Gee Whiz produce. My scalp prickled.

In the arena, Danny repeated the exercises he'd done in the pen, and added another, which was, when the horse is walking briskly around you, say, to the left, you switch the rope to the right hand (and the flag to the left), raise your right hand and give a little tug, and try to get the horse to bend toward you, shift his weight, turn, and go to the right without halting. Happy could do this at the canter—it looked like a trick. She would be cantering to the left around Danny, he would twitch the rope, she would sort of lift herself up, shift from her left hind to her right hind, and take off cantering to the right, but her canter was so controlled and graceful that she looked like a rocking horse. (Another trick he did was to walk along, leading her. He would say, "Lope!" and she would canter beside him, no faster than he was walking—I thought that was a trick Waldemar Seunig should see.) A horse who could do the turns Danny wanted could, of course, outsmart any calf or cow, but he could also maintain his balance at all times by easily shifting his weight backward and raising his front end. I won't say that Gee Whiz learned this immediately—he was much bigger than Happy, two hands and 29 percent overall—but he got the idea.

Danny handed me the lead rope, and said, "Walk him around for a bit."

He went over to his truck and came back with his saddle. He was carrying Blue's bridle, and said, "This snaffle bit is easy. Let's start with that."

"Are you going to do what Wayne does and jump up onto him?"

He ignored me.

In the end, all we did was the same exercises with Gee Whiz tacked up that we had done untacked, but the stirrups flapped and the strings flapped and the saddle creaked. Gee Whiz bucked once, but it was clear he wasn't unbroke—he knew that people do what they do, and if you are a wise horse, you go along with it the best you can. We took him back to the barn, and I brushed him down while Danny was putting that tack away. Then Danny put him in his pasture. It was getting dark—still no sign of Dad's truck. Danny helped me put the hay in the wheelbarrow, but when I rolled it toward the horses, he got in his own truck and left. He didn't say not to tell Mom and Dad he'd been there, but as it happened, I didn't. We didn't talk about Danny at all.

Truck and Horse Trailer

Farm Gate

Chapter 12

THE NEXT MORNING WAS SOPHIA'S BIG DAY, AND OF COURSE IT was a production—she showed up at nine. Her dad was driving the trailer, and she was wearing perfect clothes. When they unloaded Onyx, it looked as though Rodney had dressed him up and sent him to Madison Square Garden. Our horses weren't the ones we'd had when he lived with us as Black George, but they whinnied to him anyway, and he whinnied back. I'd expected Sophia to be kitted out, so I'd already been at it for an hour, making sure that Blue looked as good as possible, and that my saddle was soaped, if not oiled. You would have thought a trail ride was some kind of promenade.

Once we were tacked up, I pointed to the east, down between our pastures, through the lower gate, and up to the

Jordan Ranch. It was a spectacular ride, a little wild, but on good ground with flat trails. There were spots we could gallop if we wanted to. Mr. Rosebury asked how long we'd be gone, and I said, "Oh, a couple of hours."

He said, "Are you sure?"

"Well, I don't have a watch, but—"

"Are you taking any water?"

"You mean like a canteen or like a bucket?"

"For yourselves, in case of dehydration."

I'd never thought of this. I didn't know what to say, but Sophia said, "We'll be fine," in a tight voice.

We waved and headed out. The trail had dried enough to be perfect—resilient but not slippery. Onyx looked happy. He walked along with his head swinging and his ears pricked, but at one point, he sort of stumbled on an uneven spot, nothing serious, and Sophia started and grabbed mane. Then she drove her heels down and straightened her back. This was the right response—if a horse goes down, you want to be sitting up, and in good balance, but Onyx was nowhere near going down. I said, "He's been on this trail scads of times."

Sophia said, "I haven't."

In the meantime, Blue was walking along just fine. His gait felt smooth and pleasant. I patted him on the neck and tickled him at the roots of his mane. I wondered what Sophia and I were going to talk about for two hours. But I should have known. Sophia didn't need to talk—she never did. When you were with Sophia, all of the things you might have remarked on—look at the crows; the rain greened things up a bit, but the trail isn't bad at all; Onyx looks good—remained unsaid because they seemed too dopey or too obvious or, maybe, too personal (I did wonder if she was nervous, but I didn't ask). Had she done her homework? Well, of course she had. She always did her homework. How did she do on the math test? An A, of course, and if not, well, it was none of my business. So, if we couldn't talk about anything, why did I like her a little more each time I saw her?

We got to the gate into the Jordan Ranch. I sided Blue over to it and undid it, and we both went through. I locked it again. We picked up our pace as we climbed the hill, until both horses were trotting nicely, using their shoulders and lowering their heads. The hills spread to the east, and you could just see the cows and calves sprinkled black against a distant slope. They were far away, but the landscape amplified their mooing, so that it sounded resonant and deep. We let the horses pick their own pace, and Sophia did the right thing, which was to sit back a little and lower her shoulders, just because the ground could always fool you. Blue and Onyx seemed perfectly sure-footed and happy, though, and when we came to a wide, flat area, they both lifted into a canter. Blue was in the lead, but where the trail spread out, Onyx moved around him and took off.

I admit I felt a single blast of alarm, but Sophia was only two lengths ahead of me, and her body was swaying easily with Onyx's gallop. Her braids were flopping rhythmically, and her heels were deep. Blue exerted himself to keep up, and I decided to quit worrying and enjoy myself, which was easy, given how fresh and sweet the air was, and how hypnotic the sound of the horses' hooves on the trail. As soon as Sophia settled into her saddle, Onyx slowed to a trot, and Blue was right with him. We trotted for a few strides, then we walked. Everyone was breathless, Sophia, Onyx, Blue, and me, but it was the breathlessness of pleasure. The horses tossed their heads and blew out some air, and then walked along, glancing here and there. I came up beside Sophia. She did not say, "That was fun"—she would never say such a silly thing. But I did say it. "That was fun." Then, "So tell me why you finally came for a trail ride?"

She looked at me. She seemed looser and more comfortable. "Because Colonel Hawkins said it would be a waste of time."

"What does that mean?"

"What are we learning, Abby? What is to be gained? The horse is plenty fit without it. Something could happen. I would be very cautious." She spoke in a deep, measured voice, and then coughed a Colonel Hawkins sort of cough.

A few minutes later, she said, "Is this where you broke your arm last year?"

I waved toward the distant cows. "Over across there, behind those hills."

"See?" she said. "That's what he's talking about."

"I guess so."

We walked along. I didn't tell Sophia about the time I got lost and Rusty and Blue found the way home, but I looked around and paid attention to where we were. It all looked normal today. I said, "You never seem like you're afraid of anything."

She glanced at me, and said, "I guess the thing I'm afraid

of right now is what my life is going to be like if I do every single thing I'm told to do forever and ever."

Now the trail went down a hill and through the patchy shade of a grove of oaks. This was one of my favorite places to ride, though we didn't ride here very often. The limbs of the trees were rough and crooked, and we had to pay attention in order to bend our heads beneath a few that stretched over the trail. We could see a trickle of water in the stream at the bottom of the hill, and that seemed to make the atmosphere especially peaceful. There was no wind. The horses were flicking their ears, though, so I sat up and took a slightly stronger hold. Sophia said, "Look over there." The horses turned their heads. We could just see the face of a doe under one of the smaller trees, not far off the trail, maybe twenty feet from us. She was lying down, but her head was up, her triangular face turned right toward us, her dark eyes staring. I closed my legs on Blue's sides, not to kick him but to make sure that he knew that he had to keep going. I saw Sophia do the same. We passed the deer and she didn't move. A bit later, the trail angled upward, and when we looked back, we could still see her, watching us.

Sophia said, "Who is that big white horse in your pasture? He's a beauty."

"He's a Thoroughbred off the track."

"I thought so. He's got the look. I love Santa Anita."

"You've been there?"

"My dad took me one year for the Santa Anita Derby. He let me place a bet—two bucks on Lucky Debonair. I picked him because he reminded me of a horse I had then. We also went to Del Mar once. That's like going to a resort that has racing down the street. Dad gets a little excited every time they run, and Mom and I just look at our shoes, but I have to admit, that time I had the bet on Lucky Debonair, who I'd never even heard of half an hour before, I was jumping up and down and shouting his name, and he felt like he was my very own horse. Then, when they were coming back to the winners' circle after they all galloped out, it seemed like the jockey was waving to *me*. It was such fun. What are you going to do with him?"

"Train him to jump." It seemed very bold to say this, but then I said, "I know he can do it, because he jumped out of the chute I built him when a bird flew in his face."

"Are you really?"

It took me a second to say yes.

The look Sophia—Sophia!—gave me said, "Lucky you."

When we got back, it had been an hour and a half, so I had to wonder what Dad and Mr. Rosebury had talked about for all that time. Whatever it was, Mr. Rosebury was smiling and laughing the way he always did. Probably it wasn't religion.

And as the Roseburys pulled out of the gate, Danny turned in from the road. He waved to me and waited for them to go through, then he passed me, drove to the house, and parked. I closed the gate and secured the latch. Mom was already out on the front porch, and when Danny went up the stairs, she said some little thing, and he nodded, and they hugged as tight as they possibly could.

I went around to the kitchen and took my boots off, then

I waited just inside the door while Danny, Mom, and Dad talked about it. It turned out that he had taken a bus with a lot of other guys from our town to the military base up the coast. On the way back, they all compared notes about how they'd done, what results they'd received. Some of them had not passed, even some of those who were sure that they would pass. But Danny had passed. Now all he had to do was wait for his draft notice. He'd heard that would take about two months. Dad said, "You'll do fine."

Danny nodded.

We all stood there for a long, uncomfortable moment, and then Danny said, "Well, Abby, how's that big guy today?"

I said, "Sophia thinks he's quite beautiful."

Danny said, "He is." As we went out the back door, he continued, "And we are going to take it pretty slow. But we ought to be able to accomplish a little in the next two months."

All we did that morning was truly a little—the same things that we'd done on Friday, which took maybe half an hour. But I could see in Gee Whiz's face that he understood what we were getting at—he was ready to step under, ready to change his pace, his direction, his gait. Ready to be played with and attended to. Maybe he thought that his prayers had been answered, that finally he wasn't having to stand around in the pasture all day waiting for something interesting to happen. And maybe I felt the same way.

On Monday afternoon, Barbie was there for a lesson when I got off the bus—on Tuesday she and Alexis were heading back to the Jackson School. I rode Oh My while she rode Blue, and I hardly had to tell her anything at all. If it hadn't been so late, I would have taken her for that trail ride. When she got into her mom's car to go, she said, "Please come and visit!" and kissed me on the cheek. She also gave me a box of brown sugar cubes from France that her mom had bought specially for Blue. I promised to write.

On Tuesday, Danny came again and we worked with Gee Whiz again. He did a little better. He was a little more graceful. At the end, when Gee Whiz was walking around the arena looking for tufts of grass, Danny told me he wanted me to do the work for the next couple of days, just to see how I liked it. I did do it. I did like it. I liked having those dark eyes watching me, wondering what I might want. I liked having those mobile ears pricked in my direction. I liked that large presence near me. I liked the warmth of his silky coat when I brushed him. And I liked thinking about a race at Santa Anita, everyone screaming and jumping as Gee Whiz, by Hyperion, out of Tilla, by Birkhahn, crossed the finish line first.

Thursday, Danny came out to the arena as we were finishing up. I was holding the flag and encouraging Gee Whiz to trot, encouraging him to lengthen his stride. Danny leaned on the railing and watched. All of a sudden, Gee Whiz came toward me and curved around me, trotting but attentive, making a circle without there being a rope between us. After one circuit, he flattened the circle, as if he was going to trot away again, but I stepped back half a step, and he curved toward me. He went around three times, then I stepped back two steps and dropped the arm that was holding the flag. He turned toward me and trotted right up to me. I stood absolutely still and he came to a halt.

Danny said, "When did he start doing that?"

"One minute ago."

"He is really hooked on."

"What does that mean?"

"That means he accepts you. He's looking to you for instructions." He smiled. "He likes you."

"Mom said that."

"Well, haven't you noticed?"

"I did notice. But Dad says that it's only carrots and sticks."

"He *says* that. But I think he knows better. Walk toward the other end of the arena."

I did so. Gee Whiz was two steps behind me all the way. When I stopped, he stopped. When I walked on, he walked on. I made a little loop, and he followed me back to Danny. Danny said, "I'm leaving him in good hands."

"We still haven't ridden him."

"We will."

But at dinner, Dad said, "That horse going back to Vista del Canada Monday?" Monday was the sixteenth.

I put down my fork.

Danny said, "I don't think so."

"Didn't you say the other day that the racing season was beginning down south? That should open up a few stalls over there."

"I think he's better here."

"Why is that?"

Mom put down her fork.

They were sitting across from one another. Their chairs shifted simultaneously, making a loud scraping noise that caused Rusty, on the back porch, to stand up and look in the window. Danny straightened his shoulders, then said, "He's my horse, and I think he's better off here."

"You bought that animal?"

"He was given to me."

"Well, give him back. He's useless as far as I can see. Much too big."

I said, "He can jump."

Dad looked at me, then at Danny, then back at me. He said, "How do you know that?"

"I built a little chute. He did it easily."

Dad pushed his chair and set his plate off to one side. He said, "Do I have any say in what goes on around here anymore?" He got up from the table and walked out the door. Rusty gave a bark. Maybe Rusty was saying no.

A few moments later, I heard the truck start up and drive away.

We all picked up our forks again and pretended to eat, but when Mom asked Danny if he wanted more chicken, he shook his head. He looked angry, and I didn't want any more supper, either, not even the mashed potatoes, which were especially good. I had that feeling in my stomach that you get when you are getting closer and closer to the very thing that you were afraid of, except I didn't know what it was that I was afraid of. I looked at Mom. She was poking at the last string bean on her plate, so probably she was imagining that, too.

Of course, the bad thing would be saying good-bye to Gee Whiz, a horse that a month ago I had no knowledge of and no sense of, either—because that was what I would miss. Even though I'd never yet ridden him, I could, almost in spite of myself, feel that presence he had, large and thoughtful and promising, right outside the window behind me.

Danny's chair scraped. He stood and began clearing the table. If I'd ever seen him do this before, I couldn't remember it. He picked up the plates and the silverware and carried everything to the sink, where he stacked it neatly to one side. He came back for the glasses, then the serving dishes. Pretty soon Mom and I were sitting at an empty table. We didn't say anything, then Mom said, "Thanks, honey."

He kissed her on the cheek, poked me on the shoulder, and said, "See you Monday. Make sure that guy learns something tomorrow." He went out through the living room and the front door. Mom shook her head a little, then said to me, "When your dad and I got married, he told me that he wasn't going to make the same mistakes with his sons as his father had made with him and your uncles."

"Do you think he's made mistakes?"

"I think he's discovered a few things."

"What?"

"Well, the world is fallen. In a fallen world, you can't do everything right, even if you are trying very hard."

"What else?"

Now there was a long pause, and she was giving me this look that said, "Maybe I shouldn't be telling you this," but then I guess she decided that it would be a good lesson for me. She said, "When your child is so much like you, there are a lot of times that you end up arguing with yourself." She sighed. "And when you argue with yourself, how do you decide who's the winner?"

I said, "Do you think that I'm like you?"

"Sweetheart, I think you are exactly like yourself, just yourself." We stood up and did the dishes.

Friday afternoon, I made sure to do all my riding of Oh My, Nobby, and Morning Glory before I even looked at Gee Whiz, but he looked at me—I could see out of the corner of my eye that every time I took a mare out of the pasture or put one in, he would prick his ears and watch. At one point, he did go to his gate, and he did press his chest against it, and he did rattle the chain with his lips as if he knew that the chain was the key. After he did that, I led Morning Glory over to the gate and shooed him away. Yes, the clip was moist, as if he'd been working on it. I made sure it was secure and took Morning Glory to the barn.

When I was finished with her, and everything was cleaned up and I didn't have any more work for Dad to point out, I got Gee Whiz and led him to the arena. It was late in the afternoon—the shadows were long and clouds were gathering to the west. I let him go and went back to the barn to put on my rain jacket. I wasn't sure what to do with him, so I decided to let him figure that out for himself. First, he checked under the railing for grass, but I followed him, and clucked. He could eat grass anytime. So he walked along with his big, limber strides, looking here and there. I followed him at a distance. Finally, he lay down in the wettest spot and rolled, then he got up and lay down and rolled on the other side, then he stood up, shook himself off, and blew out some air. Only then did he take off running. He was big and quick. I retreated to the center of the arena to watch him. He cantered out, but he didn't gallop the way he'd done before. Every so often, he stretched his head down and kicked out with one leg, then tossed his head with pleasure. He broke to the trot, and trotted here and there, then he did what he'd done before, he looped around and trotted toward me with his ears pricked. I stood still. He trotted right up to me and stopped, his nose practically on my shoulder. I said, "No, you go away and do something," and I waved my left arm toward the end of the arena. Sure enough, he turned to look where I was pointing, and trotted away. I went after him, and stood about halfway between the center and the end of the arena, in an open area. He looped back again, and trotted around me a couple of times, his eye on me. When I turned the right side of my body toward him and slightly raised my right arm, he bent his spine so that his body was conforming neatly to the shape of the circle he was making. I was impressed. He trotted away to the left, down the side of the arena.

I turned and walked away, a little more toward the railing but still in a fairly open area. In moments, he had come back. Now he looped around and circled me again, this time to the right. I lifted my arm. He bent to carve his circle, though he wasn't as loose to the right as he was to the left. He went around me two and a half times, then trotted off. I had no idea what he was thinking, but it was really quite flattering to have this free, energetic animal attending to me. Now he picked up the gallop, went around the end of the arena, and came back in my direction. I stood still the way I knew I was supposed to, but this time it was a little more frightening, because he was really galloping. He stopped again, even sliding a little. He ended up a couple of feet from me. I gave him a pat, then I stroked him down his neck and over his flanks, on both sides. He seemed to like that.

The light was getting bluer. I walked over to the gate to get the lead rope, and he followed me, so I ended up not attaching the lead rope, only walking along, listening to him breathe and hearing his footfalls as he came along beside me. Every so often, I petted him on the cheek. By the time he was completely cool and back in the pasture, it was dark, and Dad was handing out the hay. Dad watched me put Gee Whiz away without saying anything.

The next morning was Saturday. I wondered who Melinda and Ellen would be riding in their lessons. I hadn't heard again from Jane. When I was lying in bed, listening to Simon and Garfunkel, I decided about six times that maybe I could just never mention Jane's offer again, and pretend that she hadn't said it, and then I wouldn't have to be tempted in any direction, and I wouldn't have to make up my mind. I was only in ninth grade, and I was much too young to be making up my mind, wasn't I?

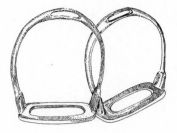

English Stirrups

Stall Door

Chapter 13

It had been a week and a half since Brother Abner's funeral, and no one had said very much about him. There'd been a little talk the previous week about Dad and Mr. Hollingsworth and Sister Larrabee going over to his place and cleaning it out, but no one had done it yet. One reason to get it done was to see whether he had a landlord, and if so, who it might be. If it was someone from far away, then Dad or Mr. Hollingsworth would have to call that person. Dad said that it was not impossible that he owned the cabin and the patch of ground that it stood on, but papers would have to be found, and maybe distant relatives? It seemed like a big job; everyone was plenty busy. When we got to church the next day, I heard Sister Larrabee tell Sister Larkin that she'd driven over and looked around for half an hour, but then had lost heart. She said, "Well, it still seems like an invasion of his privacy. You ask me, that's what relatives are for, not friends." But then Mr. Hollingsworth said that someone he knew had suggested that all they had to do was figure out the address of the cabin, and go to the county courthouse. There would be a record there saying who owned it.

Sister Larkin said, "It can't be worth anything."

Sister Brooks said, "Well, you never can tell. But what in the world would we do with it?"

Dad said, "The Lord will show the way," and everyone nodded, and then Sister Larrabee said, "You know, he had a son. There might be something about that somewhere in his things."

Every head turned to look at her. She said, "Oh, he told me about it years ago. Sad story. I was hoping it would come out as he got into his last days, but I didn't feel that I could bring it up, so I didn't."

Some of the sisters started clucking. Finally, Sister Larrabee sighed, and said, "Well, it could be there's a lesson to be learned here, and I'm sure it's one Brother Abner would have wanted us all to learn, so . . ." But it took her a long time to begin. She patted her Bible in her lap, and then she said, "Did you know he was once married? My goodness. So long ago now. Seems like that was a different world in those days. He came back from one of those trips when he was a young man, and settled down in Cincinnati, I think it was. Married a nice girl from a large family, and everything went fine. They had a boy, a healthy strapping boy, he told me, and it seems to me that Brother Abner was running a shop those people owned there in a beautiful neighborhood called Over-the-Rhine. I've been there—such lovely streets! Everything was going well, and then his wife contracted something—it wasn't the influenza, that was later, but perhaps the yellow fever? Whatever it was, it looked like she'd gotten over it, and then she took a turn for the worse, and died. Well, that boy was not even two years old, and the wife's family was a big one, several sisters all about the same age, and they wanted that boy, and Abner let them take him, for the child's own good, because how was he going to care for such a young one? But then they all had a falling-out over something a few months later, and isn't that what happens? Such a deep pain and unexpected tragedy, and then you have some little thing go wrong, and words that shouldn't get said do get said, and there you are. Well, he left Cincinnati and went all over the world again, and sometimes he wrote a letter or two to the boy, but when he went back to find him twenty years later, that boy wouldn't say a word to him, and they never made it up."

There was clucking and head shaking.

Sister Larkin said, "Seems to me that sort of thing was more the way of it in those days, but maybe I'm wrong."

Sister Larrabee said, "Well, he never figured out a way to cross back over that river, and he regretted that bitterly, he told me."

I said, "What river?"

"Oh my goodness," said Sister Larrabee with a smile. "Not the Ohio. Not a real river. It's just that when you are young . . . Well, it's the river of things that you do in your life.

241

When you're young, it's a narrow stream, but when you're old, my girl, it's a flood, and the other bank seems far, far away."

Mom, who was sitting beside me, took my hand.

Dad said, "But he took up the way of the Lord, and he is saved now, and that's the greatest thing any of us can hope for." Everyone agreed to this, and then we sang "Blessed Assurance." Church was pretty quiet, and at the end, Mom and I waited while Mr. Hollingsworth and Dad made a date to go to the courthouse, and then to Brother Abner's cabin.

When I got off the school bus on Monday, there was a nice car parked by the front porch—a red Thunderbird with lots of chrome all over it that Kyle Gonzalez would have known all about. It was bright enough to scare the horses, I thought, and then I went around the house and saw Dad talking to the exact sort of guy who would be driving such a car. He was short, and wearing a gray suit with beautifully tooled black cowboy boots, and smoking a cigar, which he kept in one corner of his mouth while he talked. Dad was kind of standing back, but he was smiling. When I got near them, I heard the man say, "Well, now, why don't you let me window-shop a little bit? See what I can see. Those are the equines over there, are they not? Let me take a look," and before Dad could say anything, the man churned across the grass toward the two pastures. Dad followed him, and I put my books down on the step and followed them, too.

At one point, Dad tried, "Now, this gelding, we call him Lincoln—"

But the man interrupted him, and said, "Pardon me for a

moment, but I just like to give them a good look. I'm easily confused, so let me look in peace, if you don't mind, just for a bit." He stuck his hands in his pockets and stood on his heels, kind of rocking back and forth. He stared first at the mares, and then he turned and stared at the geldings. It was boring. Dad cocked his head at me, so I took the hint and went inside.

Mom was looking out the kitchen window. I said, "Who's that?"

"That is Sterling McGee, from Las Vegas, Nevada."

"What's he doing here?"

"It might be that he's buying a horse."

"Why did he come here?"

"I guess he met the Carmichaels, and they sent him."

"What kind of horse does he want?"

"He said he'll know the one when he sees it."

I stared out the window with her, until it got boring again, then I went up and put on my work clothes.

But Sterling McGee did not go away for a long time. After I came down, I sat in the kitchen doing homework, because there was nothing else to do. Finally, at almost five, when Mom was rummaging in the refrigerator for the ingredients of the stew she was making for supper, we saw Dad open the gate to the mare pasture, go in with a halter, and walk around among the mares for a moment. It was impossible to tell which one he was getting, and then he emerged with Morning Glory.

We'd had Morning Glory since the summer. She was not quite a pony, and Dad had hoped she would turn out to be a

243

second Gallant Man. She was sound and willing enough, and she could jump a little, but there was something about her that was dull—it took her just a moment to decide to do what she was told, and that is something judges do not like. She also stared at cows as if they had nothing to do with her, so Dad had decided that she would probably end up as a trail horse somewhere. She hadn't cost much, she didn't eat much, and maybe that was the last time he would take Uncle Luke's word on a horse. Sterling McGee stared at her from all sides, then went over her legs with his hands, flexed her, trotted her out. Ten minutes later, Dad was bringing out a saddle and bridle, and they disappeared around the house. It was a good thing there was a clear sky and an early moon. I went out to feed the other horses. I'd just pushed the wheelbarrow full of hay to the geldings' gate when Dad and Sterling McGee came walking back from the arena. Mr. McGee was sitting on Morning Glory, and he looked fine—not terribly big. Both men had big smiles, and I heard Sterling McGee say, "I don't haggle. If it seems like a fair price, I don't mind paying it."

Dad's smile got even bigger.

McGee said, "What about this saddle? Seems to fit her. Would you take fifty bucks for it?"

Dad said, "It's pretty well broken in."

He meant it was old.

"Feels like it. Comfortable."

Dad said, "Well, why not?"

"Why not indeed," said Sterling McGee. "I'll send someone to pick her up later this week."

I threw out the five piles for Blue, Lincoln, Gee Whiz,

Marcus, and Beebop, and pushed the wheelbarrow over to the mares' fence and started throwing flakes for the five of them. When Dad and Sterling McGee led Morning Glory over, Mr. McGee stopped and petted her. Then he glanced at the others. The only thing he said about any of them was about Beebop. He said, "I like that one, too. He was my second choice. He for sale?"

Dad said, "He doesn't belong to me. He's a rodeo bronc."

"Shame. Good-looking horse."

Dad came inside a half hour later with a check for $750, including the saddle. He set it down on the table and said, "You know the name of this check?"

"What?" said Mom, stirring the stew.

"You Never Know."

We laughed.

"That man didn't look one time at Oh My, or Marcus, or even Gee Whiz, as big and white and shining in the moonlight as he is. He looked at the plainest animal in there and fell in love with her." Dad was happy all through supper, and ate not only everything on his plate, but everything in the serving bowl—Mom had to take it away to the sink and tell him there wasn't any more. After dinner, he went outside with a flashlight to check something, and we could hear him whistling around the place—as always, a sad song ("The Streets of Laredo") that meant he was feeling good.

Since, thanks to Sterling McGee, there was no riding Monday, Tuesday we had to make up for it. Danny was already there with Gee Whiz in the pen when I got off the bus. Mom said he had ridden Marcus. A trailer from the Marble

Ranch was there, too, and when I went out to find him, he said that he was taking Lady home with him—he would work cows with her for a few weeks, which was easier than bringing the calves over to our place.

Gee Whiz, who was trotting around the pen in a nice limber circle, was wearing my saddle and an English-type snaffle bridle. The stirrups of the saddle were dangling, and the reins from the bridle were looped over the seat of the saddle, then tucked under the stirrup leathers. The reins were rather loose, but secure. Gee Whiz tried to stop when I came up to the fence, but Danny flicked the flag to keep him moving. I said, "You're going to ride in my saddle?"

"That's more like what he's used to."

This was certainly true.

Gee Whiz turned, then dropped his head and flexed himself and went the other way. His hooves seemed to flash. There was a rhythm to his trot that was defined and strict, like a drumbeat, 4/4 time, sometimes faster, sometimes slower, but always even. Danny stepped backward, Gee Whiz slowed down and halted, and then Danny went up to him and slipped the reins out from under the stirrup leathers. Now he positioned himself at the horse's head, facing him, and lifted the right rein slightly. Gee Whiz stepped under immediately. Danny had him do this on the right and on the left several times, then he asked him, with just the tiniest pressure, to back up—"No problem," said the dark eyes and the flicking ears. Gee Whiz dipped his head and moved backward.

"Got your hard hat?"

I said, "It's in the barn. Why?"

"You're going to get on him."

"No, I'm not. You're going to get on him."

"I don't ride English. I'll give you a leg up."

"I don't think so." My heart was already pounding.

"I have a feeling he's easier to ride than to watch. He's nine years old, at least officially. He's been ridden hundreds of times. He isn't rank or resistant. I've hardly ever seen him buck, and he isn't built like a bucker."

I said, "He's fast." No, I'd never seen him race, but up in my room were those pictures—the field of runners arrowing toward the finish line, the jockeys huddled and holding on tight, the horses with their noses out and their ears pinned, their tails streaming behind them in the wind they themselves were making.

"You might like it. Just here in the pen." He stared at me, then smiled. "One step at a time."

I went and got my hard hat.

When I was reaching up to hold the reins and a tuft of mane, my whole body knew that I had never been on such a tall horse, but I bent my knee, Danny leaned over and put his hands around my calf and tossed me, and there I was. Gee Whiz stood still. I picked up the reins, bridging them across his neck. Danny said, "Don't hold him tight. That's the signal to go for them." I nodded and loosened my grip. Here I was, just like Ellen. I thrust my heels down and clucked.

Danny said, "That's right. He knows clucks, but he doesn't know leg pressure. Jockeys just use their legs for balance. Sit deep."

I jiggled my back a little and tried to stack myself, and

then we walked away from Danny toward the rail. Here's what it felt like—it felt like a rhythmic swinging from side to side as his long back legs stepped out. Here's what it looked like—it looked like there was an acre of horse in front of me. He was wide, too, as wide as Onyx—I had forgotten how reassuring it was to feel as though the horse is all around you, not just under you. We walked a few strides, and did some halts and turns and curving loops. I stepped him over, then stepped him over the other direction. My heart had stopped pounding, and I hadn't even noticed it.

Danny said, "Trot."

Gee Whiz trotted as if he understood the word, and why not?

The trot made the pen seem extra small, but he bent fairly well into the corners, and managed some turns. It was me who suggested we go to the arena. Danny didn't say no. As we walked there, Gee Whiz tossed his head so that the reins were looser—almost actually loose—and then he walked along kindly, stretching his body out and relaxing.

Our trot in the arena was much freer. His push was so strong that he practically "posted" me. I kept even and steady contact, but I didn't hold him tightly. The rhythm itself was what made me feel comfortable—it was so even, how could it possibly change? We trotted briskly around the arena in both directions, making several turns and loops. I was enjoying myself. And then I felt him gather his hind legs and move up into a canter.

Well, maybe Gee Whiz thought it was a canter, but Blue would have thought it was a gallop. The wind was making my eyes water, and I hadn't noticed much wind before we started galloping. I leaned forward slightly and put my heels down. I looked ahead, and I remembered that thing Danny said, "Let him go forward." I lifted the inside rein maybe half an inch, and he bounded ahead, as if from sheer joy.

I had never felt anything like it. He was not running away, and he was not pulling, but he was strong, and energy pulsed off him in waves. How many pictures had I seen from the early days of photography, when a man in California showed how a horse galloped (and lots of other animals, too)—a horse curls up his four legs, then pushes off with the hind legs, one after the other. Then his forelegs reach out—he's stretched for a moment, balanced on one foreleg—and then he curls again and leaps forward again. I felt all of that—every hoof touching the ground, every part of Gee Whiz's body reaching, then gathering, then reaching. Because there was so much horse in front of me, I felt secure. I let my shoulders and elbows follow his mouth, and my body follow the rhythm of his body.

Maybe it didn't last long. Maybe in only a minute or two he came down to the trot and I sat up and steered him back toward Danny. Maybe I was breathing hard and I could hardly see anything, but Gee Whiz dropped to the walk in the calmest way possible, as if he'd blown off a little steam, that was all.

Danny said, "That looked fun."

"I don't know. But it did feel like he knew what he was doing every single step."

"No surprise. Does a baker know how to bake bread? Does a juggler know how to keep three balls in the air? Practice makes perfect."

"We need to talk Dad into this."

"No, we don't. He said it was okay."

"He did?"

"Nothing like the unexpected sale of a horse you were kind of disappointed in to change your mood."

I said, "That was a lucky break."

Danny shrugged.

And that was what made me wonder if it was luck after all. As we were walking back to the barn, he said, "Can you skip your first class tomorrow morning?"

I wasn't an idiot. I said, "Yes."

He said, "I'll pick you up at six-forty-five."

When we got to Vista del Canada the next day, I was still yawning. But I woke up when I got to Jack's stall. He was eating some hay in the back corner, looking sleek and dark. I said, "Hey, Jackie boy!"

His head flew up, he spun around, and he rushed to the door, if you can rush taking only one step. He pressed his chest against the door, making me feel just how strong he was getting, and then he ran his nose through my hair like he couldn't get enough of me. Right then, Ike came up behind me and said, "Glad ta see ya, miss. I ain't surprised, he's a friendly kid. You get some of them who've been out in the herd most of the time, and it don't matter how often you give 'em somethin', they still keep their distance." Ike slipped the halter on and pushed the stall door open. Jack came out with his ears pricked.

Ike led Jack to the grooming area, where Danny was waiting. He handed the lead rope to Danny, and got the saddle and bridle on Jack in about two seconds. Jack behaved himself, but you could tell he knew something was going to happen, and it was something he liked.

Ike led Jack to the track, with Danny and me following. I leaned on the railing, and Ike and Jack and Danny went through, then Danny closed the gate, which wasn't a real gate, just part of the railing that moved. There were already three horses out there, finishing up their work—they must have started in the dark. Wayne walked over on his mount, a chestnut filly who was smaller and more muscular than Jack, and also mean—when Wayne brought her to a halt, she reached back and tried to bite him. Wayne just said, "Quit!" but otherwise didn't seem to react. Then the chestnut sidled her hind end around, as if she intended to kick someone, maybe Jack, but Wayne stopped her. Danny took Jack, and Ike took the filly. As soon as he had the rein, she started to back up, her head high.

Ike said, "Stop that!" She stopped. But he was careful as he led her off the track.

Wayne said, "That filly's broodmare sire line's a pain in the neck. Her broodmare sire's famous for having to wear a muzzle in the pasture, he's so vicious. Now, this one, she don't buck and she ain't sulky, but when she's not working, she wants to show you who's boss."

Danny held Jack, and Wayne did what he had done before, just sprang onto him and leaned forward, then sat up and took the reins, only then putting the toes of his boots into the stirrups. Jack was already walking forward, his ears up. He wanted to go.

But I was proud of him—he let Wayne tell him what to do, and what Wayne told him to do was walk down the track in a straight line about a third of the way in from the outside rail. After about five uneventful minutes, they eased up into the trot—they were pretty far away from me by that time, but Danny had some binoculars that Ike had given him, so I looked through them. Jack was not curled in on himself as though Ike was holding him tightly, but he did look like a spring, and Ike's reins were not loose (it would have been dangerous if they had been). Actually, Wayne had such a strong, supple seat that they looked like they were one thing, a dark being that was trotting in huge steps around the curve in the track, both concentrating on going forward, both slightly coiled, as if there was a lot of energy in there, and both under control. Of course, I had seen Jack trot all over the place (and run and jump and kick out and do everything else that a lively colt does), but I'd never seen this trot, which looked like he was made of elastic bands—giant strides, elegant strides.

They continued along the far side of the track, came around the curve, and passed us again. Danny said, "The track is seven-eighths of a mile. Wayne lets him go his own distance, but he has to go straight. That's the only thing." When they passed us, the reins were slightly looser, but Jack was still trotting out, still enjoying himself. They went around one more time, then came down to the walk again as they passed us. Now they walked around again, still in a straight line. Finally, they passed us, and then, maybe fifty yards down the track, they halted, and Wayne turned Jack toward the center of the track, keeping him there for maybe five minutes or so.

Jack stood quietly. When they came back to us, Jack was on an almost loose rein. He did not try to bite anyone when Danny took his rein.

I followed Danny and Jack over to where Ike untacked him, then I did what I'd done before, led him briskly around the walking area, stopping from time to time to let him have a sip of water. He wasn't terribly sweaty or blowing very much, but I walked him until I was told we could stop, just to be near him, just to tell him what a good boy he was, just to say how much I admired his trot and also his willingness to go straight and to keep going. And it was true, we weren't used to thinking of a lengthy trot as exciting; I knew that it was just a day's work for Jack. But I was excited.

After supper, I went up to my room and wrote a letter to Mr. Matthews. It read:

Dear Mr. Matthews,

Jack So Far has been at Vista del Canada for a month now, and my brother, Dan, who goes over there and helps with the training, or else does some shoeing, tells me that he is being a good boy and doing his work. He seems to enjoy everything about it, and it is wonderful for us to be able to go see him once in a while. I saw him get mounted the first time, and I've also seen him trot around the track. I've met Ike and Wayne, his rider, and they know what they're doing, and he likes them. Thank you for putting him in training there. I'll be sorry to see him go away from here, but I know that that is what happens with a racehorse.

My dad and mom have talked to me about what it means to have a racehorse at the racetrack. They have been told that it's very expensive, much more expensive than we thought. It would even be too expensive if we split it with you. So, I've been thinking about this, and I have a plan. I hope you will like my plan. It is this—when Jack goes to the racetrack, I will send you a thousand dollars. It's my money, and I can do this. It's also all that I can afford, or expect to be able to afford. You can figure out what sort of part this gives me in Jack's racing career. Maybe he'll win some money! I guess the horse we have now, who was on the track for many years, was self-supporting. Anyway, that's my idea. I hope it is interesting for you.

I look forward to hearing from you.

Yours truly,

Abby Lovitt

I left the letter lying on my desk, folded, but not yet in an envelope. I was one step closer to making up my mind, but only one step.

That night, I lay awake for a long time. I knew the horses were out there. I could have watched them in the pasture from my window, and there was moonlight. But I didn't want to look at them—grown-ups always said things like, "Well, you can't have everything, sometimes you have to choose," and just because they always said it didn't mean that they were wrong. Maybe in a way, I'd known for months that I would have to choose between Jack and Blue. It was only thanks to Mr. Matthews that we still had Jack, and Dad had always seen Blue as a project, just like Lester, his favorite, whom he'd sold; just like Black George, stroke of luck, was sold to Sophia; just like all the others. If I went into Mom and Dad's room right now and said, "I'll never sell Blue," Dad would start shaking his head in amazement before I even finished talking.

I decided to close my eyes and lie perfectly still. Supposedly, that was a good way of getting to sleep, but as soon as I had settled myself and was no longer rustling around, the room got quiet, and what came into my mind wasn't Blue's face, his ears pricked; it was the sensation of riding Gee Whiz—of how that big white horse lifted up under me and shot forward, his forelock floating, his mane fluttering, and his ears pricked, of how his hind legs seemed to fold under him and launch us, of how every muscle in his body seemed to know exactly what it was doing, of how he so easily carried me with him. How a horse feels when you ride him is a very strong sensation, but even though I'd ridden Pie in the Sky many times during the fall, when I thought of him, what I remembered was how he looked with Sophia on him, not how he felt underneath me. And here is what I thought—I loved Blue because I knew him and trusted him. I did not know Gee Whiz, but I felt something in him that was exciting and, maybe, irresistible.

In the morning, there was the letter to Mr. Matthews, folded on my desk. I picked it up and reread it, then I slipped it into an envelope and carried it downstairs. I set it beside my plate at breakfast—Mom saw it when she served me my scrambled eggs. She said, "I can take that to the post office." She'd already put it into her purse by the time Dad came in from haying the horses. That afternoon, I called Jane and accepted her offer.

All she said was, "The girls will be so happy!" I thought of riding down the trail at the stables—wandering among the fragrant trees, Blue's hooves quiet in the bed of pine needles, me saying something to Sophia and watching the birds, then there it would be, the Pacific Ocean, brilliant and cold and loud and strange.

I said, "I think it'll be fun, really."

Two weeks later, Mr. Matthews sent me a contract, detailing my "investment" in Jack So Far's racing career. My payment was a thousand dollars and "other consideration." My potential portion was one-third of all winnings over and above expenses, and at the end of his career, Jack would return to me. I stared at the contract, then looked out the window, wondering how he would get along with Gee Whiz.

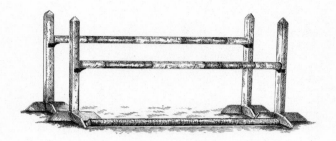

Oxer Jump

Tack Trunk

Epilogue

It's early—about six-thirty—but very light. Mom, in the front seat, is staring out the window as we go over the mountain. We saw a few lupines before we started up the grade, so she's looking for more—last year there were fields of them, just like in Alexis's painting, purple flowing down the mountainside. Even from the road, you could smell them. We don't see any, though—not quite time yet. But the hillsides are still deep green. We've had pretty good rains this winter—fifteen inches, according to Dad's little chart.

We're on the way to Vista del Canada to see Jack go for his first gallop. I haven't seen him in over a month. We turn left at the bottom of the mountain and drive past all the houses and farms. Even though there are no lupines yet, there are other flowers everywhere, including a field of irises Dad says are being grown for their bulbs. They are tall and dark purple. Mom says, "We should try to get some of those bulbs for next year. They're a beautiful color."

Danny is parked at the Vista del Canada gate. Mom and Dad and I know that he is leaving for boot camp in a week, but now is not the time to think about that. When we pull up behind him, he waves, then pushes the button. After a moment or two, the gate opens. We follow him down the long road, then up, past the upper barns, then past the fields with mares and their new foals, then down again. The track is brilliant in the morning sunshine. I can see Encantado in his usual spot, staring at the horses who are galloping or trotting or standing. He whinnies, then trots along his fence, then halts and stares again. We go around his barn and stop beside the gate of the track.

Danny jumps out of his truck. We get out more slowly. Here comes Ike, leading Jack. Wayne is beside the gate, readjusting his helmet, then his gloves. He says, "Hey there! Big day today!"

"A little big," says Ike. "Not too big."

Danny nods, Mom smiles. I try not to get ahead of myself—this isn't a race, just a day's work.

Wayne jumps on, as always. Jack stands, but he is champing his bit and picking up his front hooves and putting them back down. His ears are arrowed toward the track, and he's watching one of the other horses. As soon as Wayne has picked up the reins and put his toes into the stirrups, Ike lets go, and Jack heads out onto the track. They walk along the outside railing. Mom takes my hand. Dad says, "Well, he's behaving himself, at least."

"He ain't bad," says Ike. "Just a tad impatient, is all."

They pick up the trot. Jack is a real two-year-old now—his birthday was six weeks ago—and at the moment, he looks rather grown-up. Wayne lets Jack lengthen his trot. Mom and Dad shade their eyes with their hands and stare down the track. Jack's trot is sinuous and smooth, with big strides. Thanks to Gee Whiz, I can almost feel it. They go around the far end of the track and start up the other side. When they're almost to the second turn, I can see Wayne let out a little more rein, and Jack rises into the gallop as if he's been waiting for this all along, maybe for his whole life. Wayne holds him a little, but not too much—Jack doesn't toss his head; instead, he speeds up. He comes around the turn and passes us, dark and dedicated, enjoying himself, balanced and elastic, his strides huge and airy. Dad, Mom, Danny, and I, we can't help ourselves, we all take deep breaths and let them out slowly. Dad says to himself, "Wow."

Wayne and Jack continue down the track, again to the turn, and on the turn Jack comes to a trot again. Wayne lets him have a little more rein. Ike says, "See? Not very excitin'. Don't want anythin' to be excitin' till he wins a race. That's the way of it. We may feel however we do about it, but they got t' feel that it's all in a day's work."

Even so, Ike is grinning, and he gives me a little slap on the back. Jack So Far has been a very good boy, and that is enough for now.

About the Author

Jane Smiley is the author of many books for adults, including *Private Life*, *Horse Heaven*, and the Pulitzer Prize–winning *A Thousand Acres*. She was inducted into the American Academy of Arts and Letters in 2001. She is also the author of four other novels for young readers in the Horses of Oak Valley Ranch series: *The Georges and the Jewels*, *A Good Horse*, *True Blue*, and *Pie in the Sky*.

Jane lives in Northern California, where she rides horses every chance she gets.